I0731569

ZOMBIE GOLD

ZOMBIE GOLD

JOHN L. LANSDALE

BOOKVOICE PUBLISHING 2020

This novel is a work of fiction. All incidents and all characters are fictionalized, with the exception that well-known historical and public figures are products of the author's imagination and are not to be construed as real. Where real-life historical figures appear, the situations and dialogues concerning those persons are fictional and are not intended to depict actual events within the fictional confines of the story. In all other respects, any resemblance to persons living or dead is entirely coincidental.

ISBN
978-1-949381-22-1 Paperback
978-1-949381-23-8 eBook

BookVoice Publishing
PO Box 1528
Chandler, TX 75758
www.bookvoicepublishing.com

<u>**THE MECANA SERIES by John L. Lansdale**</u>
#1 - Horse of a Different Color
#2 - When the Night Bird Sings
#3 - Twisted Justice
#4 – The Box

<u>**OTHER WORKS BY JOHN L. LANSDALE**</u>
Slow Bullet
Long Walk Home
Beyond Imagination
Zombie Gold
The Last Good Day
Broken Moon
Shadows West (with Joe R. Lansdale)
Hell's Bounty (with Joe R. Lansdale)
Boy and Hog (Short Story)
Boy and Hog Return (Short Story)
Emergency Christmas (Short Story)
Tales from the Crypt (Comic Series)
That Hellbound Train (Graphic Novel)
Yours Truly, Jack the Ripper (Graphic Novel)
Shadow Warrior (Graphic Novel)
Justin Case (Graphic Novel)

What Others are Saying about John L. Lansdale

"Mickey Spillane fans will welcome this page-turner...Lansdale effectively delays revealing the novel's big secret until the end. Those who like their thrillers with a heavy dose of violent action will be satisfied." - *Publishers Weekly* review of **Slow Bullet**

"This is an entertaining, science fiction-historical-horror blend with resourceful protagonists and a solid cast of secondary characters."
- *Booklist* review of **Zombie Gold**

"**Slow Bullet** is a straight-ahead thriller...it's about action, and there's plenty of that. Check it out." - *Bill Crider's Pop Culture Magazine*

"...the author's innate ability to spin a complex tale painted with vivid characters and intense suspense provides readers with a well-paced book that they may find difficult to set down...a worthwhile suspenseful ride." - *Amazing Stories* review of **Horse of a Different Color**

"Has something for everyone... It's exciting, entertaining and educational. A fun ride." – legendary TV personality/actress/author Joan Hallmark, review of **Zombie Gold**

"...something unique and comfortable and difficult to put down. Highly recommended." – *Cemetery Dance* review of **Hell's Bounty**

"True to Lansdale tradition, John L. Lansdale has compiled a piece of work that should appeal to a wide range of readers."
– *Amazing Stories* review of **Zombie Gold**

"**Long Walk Home** really touched and gripped me. A great bittersweet story of light and shadow about growing up in a time gone by. I loved it." – Joe R. Lansdale

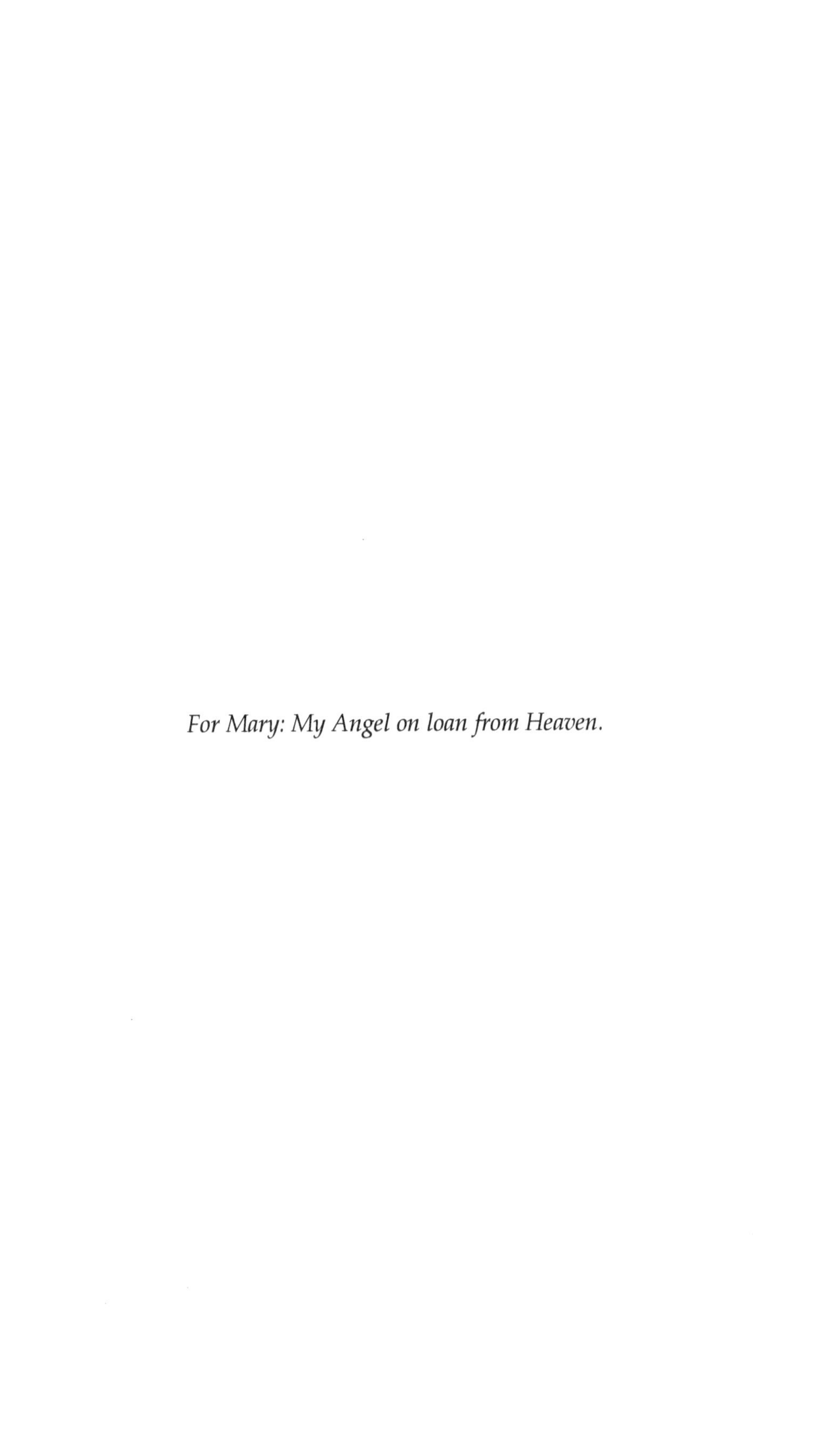

For Mary: My Angel on loan from Heaven.

For the love of money is the root of all evil.
1 Timothy 6:10 – King James Bible

1

A full moon peaked out the edge of a soft floating cloud, shining down on an iron gate with a sign hanging over it that read 'Flying G Ranch.'

A blacktop road inside the gate made its way to a large two-story, stone-covered house with four white columns. A long bunkhouse and barn were a football field length away from the house, next to a wood-fenced corral.

Inside the corral, a shadowy figure of a man wearing a cowboy hat led a big gray horse to the center of the corral. The horse was saddled and bridled. The man stopped and mounted the gray. The horse whirled and jumped, landed, and kicked both rear feet high into the air. The rider bounced and came down hard in the saddle. The horse ran and twisted his body to dislodge the unwanted rider from its back and fell against the corral fence, throwing boards in all directions. One of the boards hit the tin barn so hard, it sounded like a missile exploding and rammed a hole in it. The horse staggered to his feet, the rider still in the saddle.

A light came on in the bunkhouse, then several more. The gray took off through the busted fence up a hill, with the rider barely hanging on. The horse suddenly stopped and jumped high off the ground with all four feet. The rider went flying into the air and crashed to the ground on his back. The pain showed in his face as he sat up holding his back. The big gray walked off a few feet from the rider and stopped, lowered his head, and sniped a bite of soft dewy grass. The looped rope slid down his neck and fell off over his head. He looked back at the thrown rider like he was saying, "Take that, cowboy."

A late model Dodge pickup truck roared up the hill toward the fallen rider.

The truck stopped, headlights shining on the horse and rider. The gray galloped off across the pasture, the rope reins bouncing in the air.

Three men got out of the truck. One was a big muscular man, wearing nothing but a hairy chest, boxer shorts, cowboy boots, and hat. He had a handlebar mustache, black hair to his shoulders, and a grizzled face.

"Are you hurt, boy?" the man asked, as the other two men walked up behind him.

The man on the ground looked up sheepishly. "No, just my pride," he said. "You forget something, Sully?"

"You're in no position to be a wise guy, Chris," Sully said and reached a hand out to help him up.

"Yeah, you're right," he said. The young cowboy picked up his hat, shook the dirt off, and placed it on his head over his ruffled hair; he took the man's hand and pulled himself to his feet. He was tall and clean shaven, with a mischievous twinkle in his bright blue eyes.

"Didn't I tell you to leave that horse alone?" Sully asked.

"I had to, Sully, I had to."

Sully shook his head. "No you didn't. That's going to cost you a day's pay, Chris, and if it happens again, you're not going to work anymore rodeo stock. You're not ready for him. I shouldn't have let you on him the first time."

The other two men moved closer to Chris. One was older, tall and thin, with no hat over a receding gray hairline. A three or four day stubble covered his leather-tough face. He wore a big silver belt buckle with 'Slim' on it.

The other man was the bear of the three. He wore overalls, boots, and a cowboy hat. He made the other men look small. His nose looked like it had been broken more than once. He had wide shoulders, long arms, and monster hands. A single lick from either one of those hands could send a man to the Promised Land. "That horse has already put you in the hospital," Slim said. "You haven't been out two weeks and you're trying to go back. Trouble just kind of follows you around, doesn't it?"

"I wanted to show that nag who's boss," Chris said.

"Well, I guess we know now," Slim said. The three men laughed and Chris joined in.

"All right, the show's over," Sully said. "Get in the truck. I'll drive."

Slim and the other two men got in beside Sully. Chris got in the bed of the truck.

"Slim, you and Beebe get horses and go get Thunderbolt," Sully said. "Unsaddle him and rub him down, I don't want Chris anywhere near him." Beebe and Slim nodded yes. "I'll saddle the horses for us," Beebe said.

"Thanks," Slim said, "I owe you one. We get overtime for this, Sully?"

"Maybe," Sully said. "We got a big day tomorrow, some college boys are coming for the summer. I want you to get that horse back in the barn and get some rest, act like you got some sense when they get here. Nobody tells Mr. Goodman, his wife, or the rest of the boys what Chris did, you hear?"

Slim and Beebe shook their head yes. When they drove up to the bunkhouse, several men were waiting outside. An overweight bald guy wearing a night shirt stepped forward and confronted Sully. "What's all the noise, Sully?" he asked.

"Nothing to worry about, Cookie. Thunderbolt busted down the corral fence and got out," Sully said. "Slim and Beebe are going to get him."

"How did he get out of his stall?" Cookie asked.

"You ask too many questions. All of you go back to bed," Sully said. He walked over to Chris and whispered to him. "Chris, don't wake anyone up when you get to the house or we will all be in trouble."

"I won't. I got a key to the back door."

Sully nodded and Chris walked away.

The men began to mumble among themselves and made their way back to their bunks.

2

At six the next morning, the lights came on in the bunkhouse. Sully started running a tin cup inside a tin garbage can. The sound would wake the dead but not some of the cowboys that had been experiencing the morning ritual for several years. One young buckaroo, with a curly head of hair and tattoos all over his arms, raised up in bed and shook his head. "Man, this is worse than being in the Army." A middle-aged man in his underwear, looking like he was straight out of a Geronimo camp, grabbed a towel off his bunk and looked at the young cowboy.

"You don't have to be here, Shorty," he said. "You know it's rodeo time. Mr. Goodman has to have the stock ready to go in two weeks."

"Sully's not a foreman, Chief, he's a drill sergeant," Shorty said, and they both headed for the shower.

"Okay, Cookie, get your helpers and fix some chow," Sully said. "This ain't no slumber party. We got two weeks to get all these broncos and bulls tested for competition. I catch anyone not giving his best, he's fired. We got some new blood coming. Eight college boys signed up as wranglers for the summer. I'll let you know who gets to play nurse maid later this morning…and somebody take Walter to the shower and wake him up!" Sully yelled, pointing toward a man in bed with a blanket over his head.

The blanket flew off, and a stout-looking man with long hair and a beard opened his eyes and threw the blanket off the bed. "I'm awake, no more showers!"

"All right then, get your butt out of that bed," Sully said.

"Yes sir," Walter said and jumped out of bed.

In the meantime, Chris, James Evan Goodman, and his wife, Julie, are having breakfast in the dining room of the main house. Jim was a fourth generation owner of the Flying G. He was going on forty, not much taller than his wife, with thinning black hair, hazel eyes, and a neatly-trimmed black mustache. He wore his usual starched western

style white shirt, jeans, and custom-made python boots. His white Stetson hat hung on a rack, with a thousand dollar gold hat band on it.

His great-great-grandfather, Evan Goodman, came from England and settled in West Virginia in 1836, with two cows and a half-breed bull. He built the Flying G into the largest cattle ranch in the state. He was a typical English gentleman that had a high moral code and a stiff upper lip; meaning he could endure the rugged conditions and hardships of the time to build the ranch. Things had changed since Jim Goodman took over. He still raised cattle, but not near as many as he used to. He got into the rodeo stock business five years ago, at his wife's suggestion, and discovered there was more money to be made with wild animals than beef. His wife was a local blue-eyed, red-headed beauty from the McAllister clan that came from Scotland during the Civil War and made a fortune in the kerosene delivery business. Jim and Julie became Chris's guardians when he was twelve, after his mother, Wanda Bain, died of breast cancer. She had worked for the Goodmans as a maid all her adult life. Chris didn't know who his father was, or if he had any family. His mother said he was better off not knowing. It was rumored his dad was a young, good looking cowboy that blew in from Wyoming one winter and left the following spring, as unexpected as he had arrived. No one ever heard from him again.

"What was all the commotion at the bunkhouse last night, Chris?" Jim asked.

"Thunderbolt got out, we had to go get him," Chris said.

"Is that all?" Jim asked.

Chris looked at Julie, then Jim.

"I can't lie to you, sir. I tried to ride Thunderbolt again. I didn't. He tore down the corral fence. I'll fix it. Sully said not to tell you, he was trying to protect me."

"That horse is the best bucking stallion we ever had," Jim said. "He should bring top dollar, I don't think he can be rode," Jim said.

Julie looked at Chris. "Christopher, we don't have any children. We think of you as our own. You're probably going to own this ranch someday. I don't think your mother would be very happy with you right now. You're twenty-two years old, you have to show more maturity."

"I'm sorry I let you down."

Jim reached over and patted Chris on the soldier. "Probably would have done the same thing when I was your age. We won't let Sully know we know. He's a good man, I don't want to embarrass him."

Chris nodded and pushed his chair back. "I'll go fix the fence."

"You do that and come back up when the college boys get here. I want you to set a good example for them."

"Yes sir." Chris stood up. "Excuse me please," he said, and left the table.

3

Chris drove his Jeep to the barn and got out. He walked into the barn to Thunderbolt's stall. The horse stared at Chris.

"You think you got the best of me," Chris said. "It's not over. I know I can ride you. I'm entered in the bronco riding and when I get you there, I'll get one more shot at you." The horse shook his head like he understood. "See you at the rodeo," Chris said and walked out of the barn to the corral.

Fifteen minutes later, Slim came walking out of the barn leading a saddled Sorrel mare, with Beebe following, and saw Chris picking up ten-foot two-by-sixes to rebuild the corral fence.

"Sully tell you to do that?" Slim asked, looking at Chris.

"No, but I'm responsible for the horse tearing it down."

"I would think so," Beebe said. "Call me when you're done," Slim said. "Gives me a good excuse to postpone my butt-kicking from this mare."

Chris grinned, with a mischievous twinkle in his eyes. "I got a hundred bucks that says I can ride her," he said.

"You are a glutton for punishment," Slim said. "You ride her for seven seconds and you're on. If you do, we'll keep her for a cowpony."

"I'll say twenty you can't," Beebe said. "I'll even wear her down for you." Chris nodded yes.

"No, no help," Slim said. "He's on his own. This little gal is no Thunderbolt, but she's as wild as a March Hare."

Chris dropped the boards and started walking toward the mare when Sully came riding over a hill toward them, on his buckskin gelding. They looked at Sully, then each other.

"Guess it will have to wait," Chris said.

"Yeah," Slim said, "looks like I get to ride her."

"I'll ride her," Beebe said.

"I don't think so. You're big as she is," Slim said.

Sully rode through the barn and into the corral. "What you going to do with that mare, Slim?"

"Check her out, see if she's rodeo-tough," Slim said.

"Nope," Sully said, "she wouldn't last a week. I'm going to train her for a roper."

"She was in the Bermuda," Slim said.

"Well, she shouldn't have been. Put her in a stall and all of you come up to the house. The bus should be here any minute," he said and went galloping off.

"Looks like you dodged a bullet, boy," Slim said.

"I bet against him because you did, Slim, but I think he could ride her," Beebe said.

"Thanks, Beebe," Chris said.

"You may be right," Slim said. "You are pretty good, Chris. Sully may have saved me a hundred bucks."

"Put the mare up, and you and Beebe can ride with me," Chris said.

"Sounds good to me," Slim said.

The mini bus, with a 'Flying G Ranch' logo on each side of it, pulled in the driveway and stopped a few feet from the front of the house. The entire crew of thirty-four men, and three women, were on hand. Jim Goodman and his wife stood in the center of the big white columns, and waited for the guys to get off the bus.

The bus door opened, and eight young men of various sizes and nationalities stepped off the bus. One was an exchange student from India.

"Welcome to the Flying G, gentleman," Jim said. "We're glad you're here. I hope you had a good trip. My name is James Evan Goodman. My hands call me Jim. *You* call me Mr. Goodman. This is my wife Julie," he said, looking at his wife. She nodded to the boys and they nodded back. "Too much looking at her will get you fired. My family has owned the Flying G for over a hundred years. For the next three months, you will learn more than you probably want to. Maybe not something most of you will use later in life, but something you will remember all your life.

"How many of you know how to ride a horse?" Five hands went up. "Is there anyone that considers himself an accomplished rider?" Only two hands remained. They both looked like football players. One was a big, blonde-headed guy with a ruddy complexion, wearing a football jersey with the number 68 on it; the other one more the quarterback type, wearing jeans and a blue t-shirt, good looking, with dark hair and brown eyes, six-two or -three.

"Okay," Jim said. "Where did you learn to ride a horse, Number 68?"

"I was raised on a farm, been riding as long as I can remember," he said.

"And you?" Jim asked, pointing at the other man.

"My dad was a champion bull rider, taught me to ride before I could walk."

"What's his name?" Jim asked.

"Kirby Littlefield," he said.

"Yeah, I've heard of him. You two will help with the rodeo stock and the rest of you will work the cattle." Jim turned toward Sully.

"Step forward, Sully," he said. Sully took a step forward. "Gentlemen, this is my foreman, Braxton O'Sullivan. We call him

Sully. What he and my wife say around here goes. That means me too." Everyone laughed. "If you want to stay here, do what he tells you and do it well. We will assign a cowboy to be your partner and teach you the ropes. When you leave here, you will be tough as nails and know what it means to work hard. For now, we'll feed you and give you a bunk in the bunkhouse. There will be no drugs, no drinking, no women, no smoking, and no cussing. If you don't think you can do that, get back on the bus now." One tall, skinny guy picked up his bag and got back on the bus.

"Anyone else?" Jim asked. No one moved. "All right, enjoy the rest of the day because there won't be any days off for the next two weeks. You will work from sunup to sundown. You get room and board, and a hundred a day for as long as you last. You start in the morning at 6 sharp. If we get the stock to the rodeo on time, there will be a bonus in it for everyone. Any questions?" No one spoke.

"Sully, they're all yours," Jim said and turned to his wife. She took his arm and they walked back into the house.

4

Chris drove up to the bunkhouse, cut the engine, and got out. Sully was nearby holding a clipboard, with the college boys standing around him.

"I got your names," Sully said, "I'll pair you up in the morning with one of the hands. Cookie is a little sensitive about his cooking, so if you want to get plenty to eat, don't complain about the food. Go on in the bunkhouse, find you a bunk, and get acquainted with the boys. Dismissed," he said and walked away.

"Hey Sully," Chris yelled, "wait up!"

Sully stopped and turned to Chris. "What you need, boy?"

"I wanted to ask you if I could pair up with the Littlefield guy. We seem to be about the same age, and I think we would hit it off."

"Not to mention he might know something about riding wild horses," Sully said.

"Well, that too," Chris said.

"I don't have a problem with it if you don't get him off on the wrong track. Littlefield might be a valuable asset for you when you haul the horses to the rodeo. By the way, his first name is William."

"Thanks, Sully, I'll see that he makes a good hand," Chris said.

"I put you in charge of the shipment because Mr. Goodman said he wanted you to have more responsibility, but you got a wild streak, boy. I don't know if you're ready. You're kind of like one of those animals, headstrong and reckless."

"I'll be fine, Sully."

"Okay, I'll take your word for it. I'll assign Littlefield to you. Don't work him to death. He didn't say he was a champion rider, his dad was."

"I never been around someone that knew how the pros work," Chris said.

Sully smiled and walked away.

Chris walked back to the bunkhouse and went in. William Littlefield was putting his things in a trunk. "Hi, I'm Chris Bain," he said, "I'm going to be your partner while you're here."

William stuck out his hand. "I'm William Littlefield, they call me Will. Glad to meet you. You worked here long?"

"I was born here. My mother worked for the Goodmans before she died."

"I see. Sorry about your mother," Will said.

"It's been a long time ago. Where you from?" Chris asked.

"Kind of all over," Will said. "We traveled a lot when I was growing up. My mom and dad live on our ranch in West Virginia now. I been going to college, playing some linebacker on the football team on a scholarship."

"What you studying?" Chris asked.

"I hope to be a lawyer. I got a long way to go. What about you? Are you going to school?"

"No, this is pretty well it. I went to public school until my mom died, then Julie, Jim's wife, schooled me. She was a principal when they got married. The Goodmans are my guardians, I don't have any other family members."

"So you're kind of the boss's son," Will said.

"Kind of, but Sully is the real boss. You don't want to get crossways with him."

"I'll remember that," Will said.

"I'll show you around tomorrow," Chris said. "We have two weeks to get the rodeo stock ready. Sully said you can go with me to deliver them."

"Good," Will said.

"I'll see you in the morning," Chris said.

"Yeah, in the morning," Will said.

5

Chris met Will at the bunkhouse the next morning, and they saddled up and began rounding up the horses for riding. They had to make sure the horses were healthy and strong and had a bit of a mean streak. After Chris and Will were the only ones that could stay on a horse for more than seven seconds, the rest of the hands stopped riding and began to gather around the corral and watch them.

Walter reached in his pocket, took out a twenty, and held it out to Slim. "I got twenty that says the college kid rides the next one."

"You're on," Slim said. "That big bay is almost as mean as Thunderbolt."

"That boy comes from good stock himself," Walter said.

"We'll see how far the apple fell from the tree," Slim said.

Will led the big bay to the center of the corral. Chris grabbed the bridle and hung on while Will mounted. When Chris turned him loose, the horse started spinning around like a top, stopped and kicked at the air, and Will fell off headfirst and plowed up some dirt with his face. It was all over in less than three seconds.

Slim held out his hand and Walter slammed the twenty in it.

"Told you," Slim said.

"You try him, Chris!" someone yelled.

"Yeah," Will said, "he's a mean hombre."

"No. If you couldn't ride him, I don't think I can."

"I got fifty that says he can," Slim said.

"Me too," Beebe said.

Everyone began reaching in their pockets, pulling out money, and the betting was on. "What if Sully shows up?" Chris asked.

"He's with Mr. Goodman at the house. You're the boss now," Slim said.

Will looked at Chris. "Do it," Will said. "A couple of you guys help me hold him." Will yelled, and two hands cornered the bay and led him back out into the corral.

The men held the horse while Chris climbed aboard, got a good grip, and nodded for them to turn him loose.

The bay jumped and kicked, broke into a run around the corral, kicking and twisting, Chris hanging on.

Slim held the stopwatch, marking the time. Three seconds, five seconds, seven, then ten before Chris jumped off the horse.

"You did it, boy," Slim said. A series of laughter and moans filled the area as the money changed hands.

Will walked over to Chris and helped him up. "You're good. Maybe you should think about being a pro," Will said.

"I hope to be," Chris said, dusting himself off.

Before anyone knew he was there, Sully appeared in the corral. A devil's face focusing on the money changing hands. "What the hell is going on here? This ain't no rodeo, I ought to fire you all right now! Chris, I thought we had all this under control?"

"Sorry, Sully, I shouldn't have let it happen."

"This is going to cost all of you a day's pay and if it happens again, you're all fired."

"Sully, it's my fault," Slim said. "I was egging the boy on."

"He's a grown man, Slim. He knows better than letting the hands bet. Chris, you and Will come with me, I got just the job for you. The rest of you get back to work."

Sully marched out of the corral, stopped in the barn, and turned to the two men. "Since I can't trust you with the stock, I want you to load a truck with fence posts and wire, drive out to Kaman mountain, and replace some fence posts. I think there are about ten down. The post hole diggers and a come-a-long are in the truck. I don't want to see either one of you until that fence is fixed."

"That's a real rugged place," Chris said. "You think we can get a truck up there?"

"Hook a trailer up and take a couple of horses with you."

"It may be tomorrow before we get back," Chris said.

"Fine with me. Tell Cookie to give you some grub, I don't really want to see you for a while anyway."

"Sully, I can do this by myself," Chris said, "Will doesn't have to go. He didn't have anything to do with it."

"I don't want to send you alone," Sully said. "Too many rattlesnakes and wild things up there. Nobody has been up there for years. Wouldn't have known now if I hadn't run into a copter pilot from the forest rangers yesterday. Now I know where we're losing the cattle. The fence has got to be fixed."

"I'm as guilty as Chris is, Sully," Will said. "I was egging it on too."

"Then get to work, I'll see you when I see you. Here's the keys to the truck, the fence posts and a roll of barbwire is stacked on the other side of the barn. Take your rifles and ponchos."

"Let's go," Chris said, and they headed for the truck.

6

Chris and Will hooked up the trailer, loaded the horses, fence posts and wire, put the food and ammo in their saddle bags, and set out for Kaman Mountain. After riding along in silence for about three miles, Will spoke.

"What's Kaman Mountain like?" Will asked.

"It's a rugged place, lot of wild animals and snakes. No one ever goes up there."

"Until now," Will said and laughed. "How did it get its name?"

"A Union soldier named Ernest Kaman deserted with a band of no-goods. The story goes, Kaman and his men stole a load of gold that was being taken to the mint in Philadelphia and hightailed it back to the mountain. Would have been about twenty-million in today's money. No one knows what happened to the gold for sure to this day. Most people think someone made up the story to distract the Confederacy. The civilian guide showed up at a Union camp about two weeks after the gold disappeared, dazed and wounded, and said that they were robbed. No one believed him, but they couldn't find anything to tie him to the missing gold. They drafted him into the Army and sent him off to a western outpost. When he was drunk, he told all kinds of stories about what happened to the gold; but when he was sober, he said he couldn't remember anything about it. He died there, several years later.

"Fact is, Kaman and the other men did go to the mountain during the Battle of Gettysburg. There were witnesses to that on the ranch at the time. Kaman, his men, and the gold disappeared without a trace. Everyone started calling the place 'Kaman's Mountain' not long after, and still do. Several people have said they have seen Kaman, dressed in his Union uniform, carrying his Army issue Springfield rifle on the mountain."

"That's a fascinating story. I read about the gold missing, but I never heard that story before."

"I have been hearing about it all my life. That's the mountain you see in front of you, about a mile away."

"Maybe we will see him?" Will asked.

"You might, if you want to bad enough," Chris said.

"Never know," Will said.

"Yeah," Chris said. He paused and took a deep breath. "Will, there's something I haven't told you."

"What's that?" Will asked.

"I told you about us delivering the stock to the rodeo, what I didn't tell you was I'm entered in the saddle bronco riding. We got a horse named 'Thunderbolt' that no one can ride. I've tried, twice. I plan to give it one more go. I have been warned by Jim and Sully not to do it again. If Sully finds out, I may get kicked off the ranch forever, and you would get fired. I thought you should know."

"That's no big deal for me. I won't be here but three months, anyway. Do you really think Mr. Goodman would let him do that?"

"A very good possibility," Chris said. "Then why do you want to take that kind of chance? What is so important about riding that horse?" Will asked.

"I have to prove to myself I can do it."

"What do you think you were doing that got us into this mess?" Will asked.

"Those were ordinary nags. Thunderbolt is different. A horse like him comes along once in a lifetime. If I do ride him, I think I will be the only one that ever will. You understand?"

"I think I do," Will said. "I know that's the way my dad felt about a bull that no one could ride. Trouble with that, though, was he never did. The bull won every time. He never quite got over that. It may be the same way for you."

"I never thought about that," Chris said.

"Maybe you ought to give it some more thought. I know what it could do to you."

Chris nodded. "Yeah, maybe so. We're almost there; I'll find us a shade to unload the horses."

"Sounds like a plan to me," Will said.

Chris parked the truck under a big oak tree and unloaded the horses. They saddled the horses and stuck their rifles in the saddle holsters, tied their ponchos and saddle bags on the saddles, filled their canteens from the water cooler, sat a bucket of water on the ground for the horses to drink, and Chris locked the truck.

"If I see Kaman, can I shoot him?" Will asked, grinning. "You did say he was a deserter, that would make my great-great-grandpa happy. He was at the Battle of Gettysburg."

"I don't see why not, I don't think he will shoot back."

"What's my horse's name?" Will asked.

"The bay is named Rover, and my paint is Spot," Chris said. "I raised and trained both of them."

"Did anyone tell you those are dog names?" Will asked.

"Yes, but they can do everything a dog can do and more, watch." Chris walked over in front of the bay so the horse could see him. "Rover, roll over." The horse dropped to his knees, fell over on his side, rolled over and got back to his feet. "Good boy," Chris said, rubbing the bay's nose.

"Well, I'll be," Will said. "I never saw anything like that."

"Prop your rifle against that tree," Chris said, pointing at the big oak. Will drew the rifle from the saddle holster and propped it against the tree. Chris led the paint a few feet away, turned him around, and pointed at the rifle. "Fetch, Spot," Chris said. The horse walked over to the tree, picked up the rifle in his mouth, and walked back to Chris. Chris took the rifle from the horse and patted him on the neck.

"You must have a lot of time on your hands," Will said. "Do you know about girls?" Chris laughed. "Yeah, I know about girls. I've had a few girlfriends, enough to know the difference."

"Just don't say, you know what, when I get on that horse."

"No problem," Chris said and grinned. "We better get going."

"We should have brought some chaps," Will said.

"Too late now," Chris said. "Let's do it. We'll ride the fence line and follow it up the ridge until we find the break. I'll get the wire and tools and a couple fence posts. You see if you can tie four posts on each side of Rover, Sully said he thought there were ten down. Here's a knife. Hang the strap on the saddle horn in case you get tangled up and need to dump the posts quick. You can let me have it if I need it."

"Lead on," Will said.

7

It looked like the only thing moving in the afternoon heat was Chris and Will's horses as they followed the cow path up the mountain. A lone vulture flew down and landed in a bush nearby, to have a look as Chris and Will rode by.

"I came up here when I was sixteen, with Sully," Chris said. "It wasn't as grown over as it is now. There's an artesian well about halfway up. The cattle probably went there, then wandered out the other side of the busted fence."

"I bet that well was a big deal when this land was first settled," Will said.

"It was. Jim told me stories about the well and how his great-grandpa fought Indians and settlers to keep them from getting it. I remember seeing it, but I don't remember exactly where now." A little farther up the trail they heard water running. "You hear that?" Will asked.

"Yeah, I hear it," Chris said. "It's the well, and it's not too far from here."

They came to an opening and saw water squirting up two or three feet like Old Faithful, and spilling out on some rocks below.

"Look at that, Chris," Will said. "No wonder Old Man Goodman wanted this place.

That well must have been the lifeblood of this whole valley then."

"This is it for thirty miles if you're going west," Chris said.

Chris and Will dismounted and led their horses over to the well, and the horses started drinking from a little pool beside the rocks.

Suddenly, the horses threw up their heads and tried to pull away from Chris and Will. They pawed at the ground and stared at the bushes nearby.

"What's going on?" Will asked. "You think something is wrong with the water?"

"I don't think so," Chris said. "They were drinking directly from the well. They smell something."

There was a noise in the brush, and Chris and Will turned toward it. They got a quick glimpse at what appeared to be a man running away behind the brush. "What was that?" Will asked. "You said no one ever came up here."

"They don't," Chris said, "they think the place is haunted."

"Maybe they're right," Will said.

"That was somebody real."

"Who?" Will asked.

"I don't know, but he wasn't friendly," Chris said. "Make sure your rifle is loaded. We may have a rustler getting the cattle, and he tore down the fence to get them off Goodman land quicker. Let's drop the fence posts and find out."

Chris and Will untied the fence posts and tools, and remounted. They rode toward the brush; their rifles in one hand, and reins in the other. As they approached a big rock, a man jumped up on it, in full view. He had long, straggly black hair, sunken brown eyes, and bony cheeks. It looked like part of his nose was missing. He was wearing a Civil War Union uniform with three stripes on the sleeves, cavalry hat and boots, and carrying a Springfield rifle.

"It can't be," Chris said. "It's impossible."

"Maybe so, but there he is," Will said. "I got cold chills running up and down my back. What do we do? I got my cell, should we call Sully? "

"I don't know, he can't be real," Chris said. "Who are you!?" Chris called out. The man jumped off the rock, ran into a thicket, and disappeared.

"Do I call for reinforcements or not, Chris?"

"No, not yet, we don't want to be the laughing stock of the ranch. I got a feeling someone set us up for this. He headed down that ravine, we'll follow him."

"Not exactly what I wanted to hear," Will said.

"You can wait for me here if you like."

"Not a chance. I'm shaking in my boots, but let's go."

"That was a frightening sight, alright," Chris said, "but I think someone is playing a game with us. Sully is a big practical joker."

"I hope so," Will said.

Chris and Will rode down the ravine without seeing anyone. They came to a cave entrance about the size of a large barn door.

"What do think? Do we want to go in there?" Will asked.

"That's probably where he went," Chris said.

"You think it's Kaman?" Will asked.

"No, but I think it's someone made up to look like him," Chris said.

"Do we go in, yes or no?"

"I would like to have the last laugh on Sully," Chris said.

"I'm not laughing, but let's go," Will said.

Chris reached in his saddle bag and took out a flashlight, turned it on, and led his horse inside the cave; Will followed, leading his horse.

"Watch out for rattlesnakes, this is a perfect breeding ground for them," Chris said.

"I didn't need to hear that, either. I wonder how far it goes."

"I don't remember this," Chris said. "It looks like rain has washed the dirt away from the entrance over time and piled it at the bottom of the ravine. The entrance might not have been visible for a long time."

"Do you smell anything?" Will asked.

"Yeah, smells like something dead."

"I hope its real dead," Will said.

Chris shined his flashlight around the cave. There were bones of what looked to be humans and animals. "Something is living in here," he said.

"You're just full of good news," Will said.

"Sorry," Chris said.

A smoky haze appeared, and grew thicker as it got closer to them. "Look at that," Will said. "Where did that come from?"

"That's what we smell, it stinks to high heaven." The smoke was becoming a wall behind them. It got thicker and thicker. Chris shined the flashlight at the smoke. It was so thick now the light couldn't get through it. Images of faces began to appear in the smoke. They moaned and twisted their heads like they were trying to say something.

"You see that?" Chris asked, as he held the flashlight on the grotesque faces.

"There's something really weird going on here," Will said. "I don't know about you, but it's scaring the hell out of me."

"I'm with you, buddy. Something, or someone, is trying to keep us from getting out of here."

"I think we're out of our element, Chris. This ain't no place for cowpokes, and this ain't no game. Let's make a run for it."

From out of nowhere, Kaman appeared in front of them. "The gold is mine," he said.

"You're not taking us back and you're not getting the gold."

"Chris, I think he's real. Well, not real, but really here."

"We don't want your gold, we just want out of here," Chris said.

"This is my mountain. I'm in charge here," he said.

"Are those your people in the smoke?" Chris asked.

"Nope. I stole their gold, but it's mine now. That sickly lieutenant blabbed about the gold when we was in St Mary's. When they transferred the gold to pack mules outside of Seven Stars, we killed them all, except that coward Connors, and hid the gold there."

"You talking about the gold that was going to the mint in 1863?" Chris asked.

"That's it. When the shooting started at Gettysburg, we figured that was a good time to ride out. We dug up the gold and headed to this mountain, but the men we killed for the gold sent their spirits to take us back... but I outsmarted them. I made a deal with the Devil, to protect us and the gold in exchange for my soul, but he cheated me. We have to stay on this mountain forever. The spirits are still hanging around. They can't get me, but they can get you."

"What good is the gold if you can't get off the mountain?" Will asked.

"I'm negotiating a new deal," Kaman said.

"After a hundred and fifty years?" Chris asked.

"Has it been that long? Seems like yesterday," Kaman said.

"I don't believe you have the gold," Chris said.

"Oh no, you ain't going to trick me. It's in my secret hiding place. Not even my boys know where it is."

"There are more of you?" Will asked.

"Yep, I handpicked me enough men to steal the gold. We decided we had rather be rich than soldiers. We all wound up in this cave, and the cowards that was chasing us didn't have the guts to come in after us. They blew up the entrance and we all died in here. I made my deal and he let us out. We been on this mountain ever since. The boys will be glad you showed up, we have been hankering for a good meal for some time."

Kaman turned toward the smoke and yelled, "Come and get 'em boys!"

A ragged man appeared through the smoke, then another and another, all dressed in Union Civil War uniforms, and more kept coming. They all looked like they had just crawled out of a grave.

They were dirty and ragged. They had parts of their bodies missing; faces, arms, legs, eyes, and hair. The sound of more moans and groans could be heard in the smoke, and the sounds got closer every second.

A one-armed soldier reached out for Will. Will swung his rifle at him and knocked his head around backwards, but he kept coming. He laughed real hard and his one eye popped out.

"Holy shit," Will said, "these things are zombies."

"Run!" Chris yelled. He slapped the horses on the butt and they took off in a run, deeper into the cave. They heard a loud rumbling toward the entrance of the cave, and a wall of smoke rushed through the cave, engulfing them.

"I think that was the entrance caving in, and that's the only way out," Will said.

"We'll make a new one," Chris said. "Keep running, or we'll be dinner."

As they ran through the cave, the soldiers were in pursuit as fast as their bodies would allow. Kaman disappeared in the smoke, but they could hear him laughing. "Save me a leg, boys," he said, and started laughing again.

The sickening smell got stronger. The smoke started spinning and whirled past the soldiers, and wrapped around Chris, Will, and the horses, like a huge butterfly cocoon.

"So long, buddy!" Will yelled. The smoke cocoon kept spinning and smashed through the cave, busting out a huge hole and spinning them around and around like a tornado for several minutes, then coming to a sudden stop in an open field. The cocoon started to unwrap like a giant burrito, the faces and bodies ascending into the sky and disappearing until they were all gone.

"Where are those zombies that were chasing us?" Chris asked.

"I'm not sure, but I don't see any of them on the mountain," Chris said. "Those things got their wires crossed, Kaman said it was after them."

"He said they couldn't get him," Will said, "but that thing could get us, whatever that meant."

8

Through the glare of the sun they saw what looked like buildings about a half-mile away. They mounted and rode toward them.

As they got closer, they could see it was a small town. They rode into the town, stopped, dismounted and tied their horses to a hitching post in front of a big sign that had 'Redbud Saloon' painted on it. They looked around. There was a livery stable next to the saloon and several other stores on both sides of the street, including a small bank. People dressed in Old West clothing were on the dirt street and in the stores.

"This place looks like a movie set for a Western," Chris said.

"That's what worries me. Do we go in?" Will asked.

"Might as well. Maybe they can tell us where we are," Chris said. They walked through the swinging doors, into a room with a wagon wheel hanging from the ceiling, with kerosene lamps tied to it.

A bald-headed fat man wearing a dirty apron stood washing glasses with a rag, behind a long bar with a brass spittoon at each end. The worn board floor was dirty and stained with what looked like tobacco, whiskey, and blood.

A man and woman sat at one of the four poker tables, with a whiskey bottle and two empty glasses sitting on the table in front of them. The woman picked up the bottle and poured whiskey into both glasses, and they drank it.

Chris and Will walked up to the bar.

"Hello gents," the bartender said, "what'll you have?"

"I'll have a Coke," Will said.

"Make mine water," Chris said.

"We don't have whatever that was you ordered. I got some sarsaparilla if you don't want whiskey. And you, young man, can get all the water you want out there at the well by the livery stable.

"How about I just pay you for a glass of water and I don't have to go to the well," Chris said.

The bartender laughed. "Pay for water," he said. "You loco? Where you boys from?"

"The Flying G," Chris said.

"Yeah, I heard of it. You're a long way from home," he said.

"We sure are," Will said.

The woman got up from the table and walked over to the bar. She looked to be in her forties, kind of pretty, with brown eyes and long black hair. She had on very little make up, and was wearing a faded green dress with some cleavage showing, a few pounds overweight.

"You boys passing through?" she asked.

"Yes ma'am," Will said.

"Have a drink, it's on the house," she said. "My name's Kitty, I own the place." Will and Chris did a quick double-take at each other.

"You're kidding," Will said.

"No, I own it. Most people are surprised when they find out a woman owns a saloon," she said.

"That's not exactly what we were thinking," Will said.

"Leave it alone, Will," Chris said. "Miss Kitty, we just got into town and we don't know where anything is. In fact, we don't even know what day it is."

"Sunday, the 28th of June, 1863. And this is Morganville," she said.

"Did you say the year was eighteen sixty-three, ma'am?" Will asked.

"Yes. Are you boys drunk?" she asked.

"No, ma'am," Chris said. "Thank you for the offer, but we'll just get some water from the well."

The man that was sitting with her had gotten up, and was eyeing Chris and Will as they walked out of the saloon. He looked to be six-foot-four or more, about the same age she was, with broad shoulders and a Colt strapped low on his gun belt, the holster tied down. He had a star pinned on his shirt.

Chris and Will walked outside to the hitching post and untied their horses. "I read about this place in the history books," Will said. "It may be 1863. Kaman said take him back, maybe he meant in time. This town sprung up during the Civil War when all the troops from both sides was traveling through, then disappeared around the turn of the century. If I remember my geography, we're about thirty miles from the ranch, and twenty-five miles from Gettysburg. Three days away from the biggest battle in American history, in a hell of a mess. I wonder why that thing dumped us here."

"Beats me," Chris said. "May be where it was supposed to take Kaman. I'm still trying to figure out if I'm dead or alive."

"I think we're alive, but we may be in the middle of the Civil War," Will said. "Let's get that drink of water before I hyperventilate." Will led Rover over to the well, Chris followed with Spot.

Just inside an open-door livery stable, a huge man built like a tree trunk wore a leather apron over his overalls, and was hammering on a horseshoe with a big hammer.

They stopped at the well in front of the livery stable and let the horses drink from a water trough.

Will let the bucket down the well and drew a bucket of water up. Chris picked up a gored dipper, dipped it in the bucket, took a big drink, and handed it to Will.

The big man laid his hammer down and walked out to the well. "Hello boys," he said. "You need to board your horses? I got plenty of hay and grain, fifty cents a day."

"No sir," Chris said, "we're going to be moving on."

"Name's Max. People call me Brute."

"I'm Chris, and this is Will." The huge man stuck out his hand and they both shook hands with him.

"Where you headed?" he asked.

Chris looked at Will and shrugged his shoulders.

Chris looked back at Brute. "We don't know for sure yet. We're cattle buyers, looking for a heard to buy."

"We're what?" Will asked, twisting his head.

"I thought something like that," Brute said. "Them new duds you got on and them fancy saddles are too rich for a cowboy's blood. Afraid you're out of luck with the cattle. The Army done bought most of the cattle. You could sell some, but I don't know of any for sale. The war's turned everything upside-down. Lots of bushwhackers running around, better watch out for them."

"We will," Chris said.

"If you're headed west and the Army sees you, you might wind up a soldier. There's talk of Lee and the whole Reb Army coming this way. General Hooker's going to need all the bodies he can get."

"Oh no...it is 1863," Will said.

Brute looked at Will. "You don't know what year it is?"

"We do now," Will said.

"Thanks for the advice," Chris said. "We better be going."

"You're welcome. If you're back this way, stop in," Brute said.

"We'll do that," Chris said.

As they rode out of town, people were staring at them like they had two heads, including the marshal.

"Where are we going?" Will asked.

"I don't know. I just thought it was time we got out of there before that marshal started asking questions we can't answer."

"Cattle buyers?" Will asked. "Where did you get that one?"

"We had to tell him something," Chris said, "what did you want me to say? 'Excuse me, we seem to have took a wrong turn about a hundred and fifty years in the future, could you tell us how we get home?' Besides, we do sell cattle to the Army, I sold a bunch last month."

"Okay, sorry, we're cattle buyers. We're still in the same general area as we were before the unbelievable happened. Maybe we can find the mountain and the cave. I'm not too anxious to tangle with those zombies again. If they bite you, you turn into one, but if that's what we have to do to get home, so be it."

"That's what you see in the movies," Chris said.

"How do you know it's not true? I didn't think there was zombies either, but there is. Those things have been there for a hundred and fifty years."

"We're going to have to go through them to get back," Chris said. "If it's 1863 and the story about Kaman is true, none of them will be there until they steal the gold. We could go back, but what then? I think the only way we can get back to our time is to be with Kaman when he goes to the mountain, after he steals the gold. Being there beforehand may change the sequence of things that have already happened, and we'll spend the rest of our life here."

"I see your point. You're a pretty smart fellow, but we still won't know if it will work until it happens."

"Exactly," Chris said. "Kaman said they picked up the gold when the shooting started at Gettysburg. I think he meant the 1st of July, and headed for the mountain. We got three days to find Kaman somewhere between Gettysburg and the mountain, mixed in with thousands of soldiers. He said they hid the gold at Seven Stars. We have to be there before he gets there, then follow him back to the mountain. If either army finds us before then, they may shoot us as spies, so it may not matter anyway. I keep thinking it's all a bad dream and I will wake up any minute."

"I thought you were taking this way too calm. Now I know you're a basket case just like me. Let's see if there's anything in the saddle bags fit to eat. Get some rest, and try to figure this thing out in the morning."

"I am hungry," Chris said.

9

They found a spot not too far off the wagon road, with several trees to block out the moonlight and conceal them. They tied the horses to a rope they stretched between two trees, and bedded down for the night next to each other; their rifles beside them, their heads on their saddles. Chris propped his head up on his elbow and looked at Will. "What you thinking about?" he asked.

"The same thing you're thinking. What's going to happen to us?"

"What if you have to shoot someone?" Chris asked.

"I don't want to, but if it's me or him, it's going to be him."

"I'm sorry I got you into this. If I had left that horse alone, none of this would have happened."

"Not your fault, I'm a grown man. I don't think anyone will top my 'What I Did Last Summer' essay if I get back to school."

"I see you still have your sense of humor. You're going to need it."

"When we don't come home in the morning, I bet everyone on the ranch will be going nuts trying to figure out what happened to us," Will said. "I wonder what they will do if they see Kaman?"

"That rumbling behind us as we were running through the cave sounded like the cave was falling in, or maybe the entrance closing up. Kaman and his bunch may be trapped in the cave."

"I'm sure they're still there waiting on us. What are you going to do if we can't get back?" Will asked.

"I'll probably go back to the Flying G, at least that's going home in some way. Only family me or my mother ever had. What about you?"

"I do have a family, and I'm going to miss them. But if I can't go back, I think I'll go in the Army. My family has lots of soldiers in their history. I've done a lot of research on the Civil War because of my great-great-grandpa. That would be the closest family thing for me. I was named after him, Colonel William Samuel Littlefield. He was in the battle at Cemetery Ridge and lived to tell about it. I might even meet him, how cool is that. Might as well add my name to the list and hope I survive too; although, I won't be born for another hundred and thirty years…or will I?"

"I think this is it. We just get one shot," Chris said.

"Might've known I would blow it."

"I thought you were going to be a lawyer? You got some training, all you would have to do here is say you're a lawyer and hang out a shingle."

"I know, but I was having second thoughts about that anyway. If I do get back, I think I'll still go in the military. I've been enrolled in the ROTC program for the past year, so it's not something that just occurred to me. Don't have any desire to ride wild animals like you and my dad."

"It was that particular one, we had a kind of love-hate thing going. He's a magnificent animal. I'll never know, now."

"I don't know; something brought us here, maybe something can take us back. The impossible has happened, might as well think it can happen again."

"I'll try to keep that thought, although I don't think we have much of a chance."

"You do that. Think about riding that horse. You got some unfinished business back there, don't be the Prophet of Doom."

"Just telling the truth. Goodnight, Will."

"Goodnight, Chris."

10

Gun shots woke Chris and Will as the sun was crawling over the trees.

"Where did that come from?" Will asked.

"Somewhere down the road, I think," Chris said. "We better get the horses saddled quick."

They got up, saddled their horses, and rode along inside the tree line for cover a ways before they saw where the shots were coming from. A man and two women were crouched down behind a rock, three men in Union Army uniforms were shooting at them from a ledge on the other side of the road. "They got them pinned down," Will said.

"What do you think we should do?" Chris asked. "You're the one that wants to be a soldier."

"Well, we can't let them get killed," Will said. "I'll see if I can get behind the ledge, and when I wave, you start firing. When they come up to fire at you, I'll put several rounds around their heads and maybe that will scare them off."

"And if it doesn't?"

"This ain't Gunsmoke, it's for real."

Chris nodded. "Go," he said.

Will tied his horse to a bush, sneaked up the back of the ledge, moved into a position to see the three men, and waved at Chris. Chris raised up and started shooting over their heads. The men saw Chris and turned their fire toward him. He ducked down behind a rock.

Will bounced four quick rounds off the rocks above them. One of them yelled to the others. "There's a bunch of them! They got us in a crossfire, let's get out of here!" They ran to their horses, mounted, and rode away in a cloud of dust.

Chris yelled from the cover of the rock. "We're trying to help, we're not going to hurt you! We're coming out."

Chris got up, dropped the barrel of his Winchester to his side, and walked out from behind the rocks. Will came across the road and joined Chris. What they thought was a man was a boy, maybe thirteen or fourteen, and two women, one not much older than the boy. The boy had on a homemade gray shirt and high-water brown pants tied around his waist with a rope and no shoes. The women were wearing long cotton dresses and bonnets.

"Thank you," the older woman said to Chris. "They surprised us. We had stopped for the night and was fixing breakfast when they came riding up, shooting at us. The horses bolted and ran off with the wagon, our rifle in it. Thank god you and your friend came along, or we would be dead. My name's Cynthia Woodberry, and this is my son, Gilbert, and daughter, Liddy."

They both nodded a hello but didn't say anything. Chris and Will could see their resemblance, all of them had blonde hair and blue eyes.

"I'm Chris Bain, and this is Will Littlefield, ma'am."

"This is a dangerous place, ma'am," Will said. "What are you doing out here?"

"We're on our way to meet up with my husband. He's in the Army with General Hooker, in Maryland."

"Ma'am, you should turn back. There's going to be a big battle at Gettysburg soon. It's no place for women and children," Will said.

"We got no place else to go. The Rebs burned our house down and took everything. We barely escaped with a few things and the clothes on our backs before they got there."

"Where was that?" Chris asked.

"Farris Crossing, about twenty miles north of here," she said. "How do you know there's going to be a battle at Gettysburg?"

"I just do," Will said. "It's going to happen kind of by accident. The Union will win."

"He's right, ma'am," Chris said. "You shouldn't go there now."

"Are you some kind of spies?" Liddy asked. "My daddy wrote us a letter last month, and he didn't say anything about there going to be a battle there. He's a colonel, he would know."

"Like I said, it wasn't a planned place for a battle, it just turned out that way when both sides showed up at the same place at the same time, and it grew from that."

"Ma'am, you'll never make it," Chris said. "There's too many men out here like the ones we ran off."

Gilbert stepped in front of Chris and looked him straight the eye. "I would have killed them all if the horses hadn't have run off with my rifle," he said.

"We got no place else to go," Cynthia said.

"Excuse us a moment," Will said. He took Chris by the arm and they walked several yards away. "There's no way they will survive that trip by themselves. They don't even know to get off the road to camp. I think we should ride along with them to a safe place."

"Why the Good Samaritan act all of a sudden? Would it have anything to do with that pretty little girl?"

"No, they need us."

"What makes you so sure we will survive?" Chris asked. "We may get killed before they do. You don't have any way of knowing what we will be up against. We're not in the history books, we're playing this by ear."

"If someone attacks us, they will be in for a big surprise," Will said. "We can fire ten times as fast as most of the rifles here. There are some Spencer Repeaters, but not many. The Army didn't order them for the same reason most government things get screwed up, politics. There's nothing like these Winchesters. They call the 1873 model 'The Gun that Won the West' for good reason, and we got two reproductions of them."

"You're not too good at arithmetic are you? If there's two or three, sure, provided we can acquire some .45 rounds somewhere for the Winchesters. But if there's more than that, it's 'Katy, bar the door!' for all of us, I only brought one box of .45s."

"I know, but I'm going with them. I couldn't live with myself if I didn't."

"You may not anyway."

"You coming or not?" Will asked. "You going to continue being the Prophet of Doom, or are you going to do something right and good?"

Chris stared at Will for a second or two. "If we don't find Kaman in time, we are doomed to spend the rest of our life here, which will probably be very short. But I hear you. Go tell them we'll go with them. I'll ride down the road and find the wagon and horses, if the bushwhackers didn't take them. I hope they got something decent to eat in that wagon, I'm still choking on Cookie's peanut butter and jelly sandwiches."

11

Will walked back to Mrs. Woodberry. "Ma'am, we'll tag along if it's okay with you. Chris is going to get your wagon."

"That's very kind of you, but we wouldn't want to put you out," she said.

"No problem," Will said. "We're all going the same way."

Liddy and Gilbert were listening to what Will said, and confronted him. "How do we know you're not up to no good?" Liddy asked.

"You don't, but we're not. This is no place for women and children to be by themselves."

"I'm no baby," Gilbert said, "I can take care of my family. If you would fetch our wagon, that's all the help we will need."

"Mr. Littlefield," Cynthia said, "my son means well, but he doesn't understand the dangers. I accept your offer. My husband will be glad to pay you for your trouble when we get there."

"That's not necessary, ma'am," Will said. They heard a rumbling of wagon wheels, and saw Chris come in to view with their horses and wagon.

"He found them," Cynthia said. "Thank god."

Chris rode up to them, leading the horses, and stopped. "Looks like the horses took off one way and the bushwhackers the other," Chris said. "I found them chewing on some sawgrass near a creek, about a mile down the road."

"That creek sounds like a good place to have that breakfast we started," Cynthia said. "You boys hungry?"

"We sure are," Chris said.

"All right, kids, get on the wagon and let's get going," she said.

Liddy and Gilbert climbed up on the wagon, while Chris and Will led the way. After a good breakfast of pancakes, molasses, and salt meat, Chris and Will walked off a ways to talk.

"We might do better if we just traveled at night, with all the trouble going on," Will said.

"I don't think we can do that," Chris said. "Takes us too long to get there, and we have our own agenda we have to worry about. I took a look in the wagon before I brought it back, and they don't have more than three or four days of food left. That will be two if we eat any more. They have a sack of grain for the horses, so they should be okay there, long as we can find water. I saw six shells for that old single-shot Remington rifle. There was a loaded Colt .45 and gun belt under a blanket. I think Mrs. Woodberry has that in case worse comes to worse, if you know what I mean."

"Yeah, I know what you mean," Will said. "There's going to be skirmishes between the North and South along the way. I think I remember my history well enough for us to avoid the areas, if I can remember the right dates. She said her husband was in General Hooker's command, but that has already changed. Hooker will resign today, and President Lincoln will give the command to General Meade. I don't think that will affect her husband."

"We should keep moving and just stop for rest when we have to," Chris said. "Time is getting short. If they have some money, we can get supplies at the next place we come to. I'll let you ask them, since this was your idea."

"You're all heart," Will said.

"While you're at it, we could use some ammunition."

"I'll see what I can do," Will said. "Liddy already thinks we're out for no good."

"What was that you were saying, about 'you have to do what you have to do?'"

"I talk too much," Will said.

"I'll move on up ahead and keep a look out, you stay with the wagon," Chris said.

"That's called riding point," Will said.

"Okay, General, that's what I'll do."

Will smiled, and walked back to the wagon. Chris mounted and rode off down the road.

As Will walked back to the wagon, Liddy was eyeing him like she was expecting him to turn into the Devil at any minute. It made him very uncomfortable. Asking for money was the last thing he wanted to do.

"Did you get enough to eat, Mr. Littlefield?" Cynthia asked.

"Yes ma'am," Will said. "Please, call me Will."

"Very well," she said. "And you can call me Cynthia. I saw Mr. Bain ride off ahead, are we ready to move on?"

"Yes ma'am."

"Kids, get in the wagon, time to go," she said.

"Ma'am," Will said, then paused.

"What is it, Will?" she asked.

Will looked at Liddy. She was still giving him the evil eye.

"Nothing. We'll talk later," he said, as he untied Rover from the wagon and mounted.

Liddy and Gilbert got in the wagon. Cynthia untied the reins from the wagon, climbed up on the wagon seat, released the brake, tapped the reins on the horses' backs, and the wagon wheels began to roll.

12

Chris came galloping up and stopped beside Will. Mrs. Woodberry pulled up her horses and stopped behind them.

"There's a train depot and a trading post not too far up ahead," Chris said. "We can get supplies and ammo there. Maybe they can sell the horses and wagon, and we can put them on a train and get on with our problem."

"I haven't asked her yet," Will said.

"Why not?"

"It's not easy. Liddy still suspects we're going to kill them or something. I've been trying to get on her good side."

"We don't have time for you to worry about what a teenager thinks, talk to Mrs. Woodberry...now. That may be the last place before all hell breaks loose."

"Okay, I'll do it." Will turned his horse around and rode up beside the wagon. Liddy and Gilbert were sitting beside their mother on the wagon seat.

"Cynthia," Will said, clearing his throat, "Chris has found a place for supplies. I hate to ask you, but we're broke. Do you have any money? We need food and ammunition."

"See, Mama," Liddy said, "I told you they were up to no good. He wants to know how much money you got so he can steal it all."

Mrs. Woodberry looked at Liddy with a stern expression. "Hush, young lady. I have fifty dollars, Will, how much do you need?"

Chris sat on his horse in silence, while Will did the talking.

"That's a lot of money for this time and place. I think ten would be more than enough. You pick out what we need to eat; Chris and I will get the ammunition. You pay for it, we don't want any of the money."

"I bet you don't," Liddy said. Mrs. Woodberry gave her a mean look, but didn't say anything to her.

"I can do that," Mrs. Woodberry said. "I think you should know I have my husband's Colt .45. I want one of you boys to take it; I'm not much of a shot, and I think you could do better with it if we're attacked again."

"Yes ma'am," Chris said. "Give it to me, I'm a pretty good shot."

Mrs. Woodberry reached behind the wagon seat and pulled the Colt from under a blanket and handed it to Chris.

"You shouldn't have done that, Mama," Liddy said.

"Will you hush, child. I know what I'm doing. If these boys meant us any harm, they would have already done it."

Will looked at Chris. "How come you get it? I can shoot too."

Chris stepped down off Spot and strapped the gun belt on, tied the holster down on his leg, and checked the cylinder. "Set one of those empty cans in the wagon on that rock over there, Will, and I'll show you why I should have it."

Will picked up a can from the wagon and walked over to a big rock about twenty feet away, set the can on it, and walked back beside Chris.

Chris smiled, slowly lifted the pistol halfway out of the holster, then let it slide back in. Before anyone knew what was happening, he drew and fired. The can flew up in the air and he put another hole through it, before it hit the ground. He twirled the pistol around and dropped it back in the holster.

"That's why I should have it," he said. "I was the Quick Draw champion three years in a row at the state fair."

"I never saw your hand move," Will said. "That's the fastest draw I ever saw."

"That was amazing, Mr Bain," Gilbert said. "Will you teach me how to do that?"

"You're a might young. I don't think your mother would approve."

"No, I wouldn't," Mrs. Woodberry said. "I guess that settles that," Liddy said. "I think we know who should have the gun now," Mrs. Woodberry said.

"You got no argument from me," Will said. "Let's get going."

"Told you," Chris said.

"How was I to know you were Wyatt Earp?"

"You can be my Tonto," Chris said, laughing.

"No thank you," Will said.

13

"Follow me," Chris said.

Will waited until the wagon rolled off, and fell in behind.

The trading post was an old long log building, next to a small depot, with a train platform and railroad tracks on the other side. Two men were loading boxes onto wagons in front of the store. One was a muscular young man in his twenties, with black hair and brown eyes. The other one was older, with similar features.

When they walked in the store, a tall man with long black hair and a beard was placing items from the counter into a bag. He looked a lot like the other two. Chris and

Will stood on each side of Cynthia. Gilbert headed for the candy, and Liddy went to the cloth.

"We need supplies," Chris said.

"We're closed," the man said. "The Rebs will be here by nightfall, and we got to get our stuff and get out of here."

The men who were loading the wagons walked up to the doorway and stood there, with rifles pointed at them.

"How do we know ya'll ain't Johnny Rebs?" the tall man asked.

"My husband is a colonel in the Union Army, he's at Union Army headquarters in Maryland," Cynthia said. "That's where we're going."

"Who's these hombres?" he asked.

"They're friends of mine. They're helping us get there. This is Chris on my left, and Will on my right."

"We don't need much, just some food and some .45 cartridges," Will said.

"We're closed. Go somewhere else," the tall man said.

"Mister," Chris said, "all you have to do is let us pick the stuff out, and we will pay you and be on our way. We could get it while we're standing here talking about not getting it."

The tall man eyed the Colt on Chris's hip. "I don't want no trouble. Go ahead, but put all of it right here in the middle of the floor where I can see it before you take it out, and I'll let you know how much you owe me."

"We'll hurry," Cynthia said.

"Sorry ma'am, didn't mean to be so cankerous, just worried about losing my goods. My name's Jeb Musgrove, and the two standing in the doorway are my brother, Rupert, and his boy, Boone." The two men lowered their rifles and walked back outside.

"Cynthia," Will said, "if you and the kids will get the supplies, Chris and I will get the ammo and feed and water the animals. You better hurry, considering what the man said."

The two men that were loading the wagon came back in the store. "Jeb," Rupert said, "we ain't going to have enough room in the wagons for everything. We need another wagon."

"I don't have another wagon," Jeb said.

Chris looked at Will. "You thinking what I'm thinking?" Chris asked.

"Yes. I'll find out." Will walked over to Cynthia. "Ma'am, I think there may be a better way to get to your husband than the wagon."

"What's that?" she asked.

"The storekeeper needs another wagon, and Chris and I thought maybe you could sell your wagon and horses to him, then you and the kids get on a train. It would be quicker and safer than what we're doing. You could buy you another wagon and horses when you get there with the money you get for these. We should be able to telegraph Union headquarters to let your husband know you're coming. What do you think?"

"I am awful tired, and I know the kids are. If we can make a deal, and there's a train going to Maryland, I think that would be fine. Why don't you see if you can get a fair price for me? I think he would deal better with a man."

Will noticed Jeb was listening. "I might be interested if the price is right," Jeb said.

"I'll see what I can do," Will said. "Let me check at the depot and make sure there's a train going there first."

Cynthia nodded her head. "I'll wait."

She sat down on a sack of flour, and Chris and Will walked out of the store to the depot. A scarecrow-thin old man, wearing overalls and a railroad hat with the name 'Charlie Smith' sewed on the bib, was standing on the train platform, with a red flag in one hand and a green flag in the other, looking down the track.

"Is there a train going to Union headquarters in Maryland today?" Chris asked.

"There's one due any time now with a load of soldiers. May be the last one for a while with Lee's Army coming this way. I'm waiting to signal them if it's alright to stop. It looks like it will be. If you want on, it's a dollar a piece."

"You think it would be safe for a woman and two kids to get on that train?" Will asked.

"We got conductors on the train. I think it would be all right, if they don't mind the soldiers."

"Would you telegraph General Meade's headquarters?" Will asked. "I need to let her husband know they're coming."

"I don't know how to get in touch with them, but they got a telegraph operator on the train that will."

"Good," Will said, "we'll be right back."

Will and Chris walked back to the store.

Jeb was standing at the door looking at his wagons.

"I don't think we can get another thing on them, Jeb," Rupert said.

"We won't have any of it if we don't leave before the Rebs get here."

"I think we got a solution for you, Jeb," Will said. "Mrs. Woodberry will sell you her wagon and horses and catch a train if you want to buy them. You give her a fair price, and throw in some ammo and food for her trip, and we got a deal."

"How about twenty dollars, and two boxes of shells," Jeb said.

"How about a hundred, and four boxes of .45s," Will said.

"That sounds awful cheap," Chris said.

"Cheap," Jeb said, "that's highway robbery."

Will glanced at Cynthia, and she smiled.

"Excuse us for a minute, Jeb," Chris said and took Will by the arm, walking him over to a corner. "Do you know what you're doing?" Chris asked.

"Yes I do. In 1863, you could buy the best horse in town and a saddle for fifteen bucks," Will said, and Chris nodded.

They walked back to Jeb. "We talked it over. A hundred dollars and the four boxes of ammo, Jeb, that's it. Take it or leave it."

"I got no choice, I'll lose three hundred if I don't," Jeb said.

"You hear the deal, ma'am?" Will asked, looking at Cynthia.

"Yes, that's fine," Cynthia said. "We have to get our things out of the wagon."

"Looks like we got a deal, Jeb," Will said.

"Okay, get what you need and I'll get your money," he said.

"I want some peppermint sticks," Gilbert said.

"I want a roll of that velvet so you can make me a dress, mama," Liddy said.

"The man said get what we needed, not what we wanted," Cynthia said.

"Please, mama, please," Liddy said, "it's so pretty."

"Oh, alright," Cynthia said. "Both of you get what you want and I'll pay him for it."

"That's all right, ma'am," Jeb said. "I couldn't help but overhear you. Might as well throw that in too."

"Why, that's right kindly of you, Mr. Musgrove," Cynthia said.

After Jeb gave the Woodberrys their money and they got some food, they put their things in tow sacks and sat down on a bench by the depot to wait for the train. Chris and Will put their ammo and food in their saddle bags and put the feed bags on their horses. They heard horses coming and three riders rode in, dressed in Union Army uniforms, carrying Springfield rifles.

A big man with no hat and dirty blonde hair rode up close to a wagon and looked in. He had sergeant stripes on his sleeves, with a new Navy pistol stuck in his belt.

"Who owns these wagons?" he asked.

"I do," Jeb said and jumped down from the wagon. "What can I do for you boys?"

"We're going to commandeer these Wagons for the Union. You got any problem with that?" he asked.

"Yes I do," Jeb said. "You got no right to take my wagons."

"Well, we're going to," he said.

Rupert grabbed his rifle, but before he could fire, the sergeant shot him dead with his Army pistol. "Don't touch that Colt, mister," he said, pointing his pistol at Chris.

Jeb ran to his brother and took him in his arms. "You killed him," he said. "You didn't have to kill him," Chris said.

"What was I supposed to do, let him shoot me," the sergeant said. "You're not soldiers," Will said.

"We're not getting killed for some fancy-pants officer," the sergeant said. "We do what we want to now. Get off the wagon, boy, or you're next," he said to Boone. Boone jumped off the wagon, and ran to his dead father and Jeb.

Jeb jumped up and ran toward the sergeant, screaming, and tried to pull him off his horse. The sergeant slammed the barrel of his pistol hard against Jeb's head, and he went down, blood flying, and didn't move.

"The rest of you behave yourself, or I'll kill you too," the sergeant said.

The two other men were more interested in Cynthia and Liddy than the wagons.

One of the men was snaggle-toothed, with a filthy beard, and looked dumb as a rock. The other one had beady eyes like a snake, and kept flicking his tongue out at the women.

The station master came out of the station and yelled at the two men. "Leave them alone!" he said, and led them inside the depot.

Snaggle Tooth laughed and rode up beside the sergeant. "Hey Sarge," he said, "that's them pretty ladies we almost got."

"Shut up, Boyd," the sergeant said. "You and Carter get on a wagon, I'll lead the other one out of town so I can watch these citizens if they try to shoot us."

"That's the same ones," Will said.

"I know," Chris said.

"Shut up, you two," Sarge said. "I'm going to take that little girl with me, Sarge," Snaggle Tooth said.

"We don't have time for that now. Get on the wagon like I told you."

"We ain't in the Army no more, I'll do what I want to," Snaggle Tooth said.

"No you won't," Chris said.

"What was that?" Sarge asked. "I'm holding a gun on you. We'll do whatever we want to or we'll kill all of you. In fact, I think I'll start with you, pretty boy. I like that gun you're wearing, and it looks like you don't know what to do with it."

Sarge shifted in the saddle to fire his pistol at Chris. Chris drew and fired three times. In less than a long second, all three men lay dead on the ground, with a bullet through their heart.

Chris stood motionless, looking at the dead men, the Colt dangling in his hand.

"I didn't want to do that," he said. "He left me no choice. I think I'm going to be sick." He holstered the Colt, bent over, and threw up.

Cynthia ran to Jeb and lifted his head up, ripped a piece of her petticoat off, and wrapped his blood-soaked head. He began to move and she sat him up.

"Where'd they go?" Jeb asked.

"Chris killed all three of them," Cynthia said.

"He did? Is Boone okay?" he asked.

"Yes, he's fine, he's with your brother. He didn't make it. I'm sorry."

"Yes, I remember what happened now. We have to get out of here as fast as we can, before more come."

"Yes we do," Cynthia said.

Chris was still staring at the dead men on the ground. Will put his hand on Chris's shoulder. "They would have killed us all and took the women," Will said. "You're our 911. That gun, and your ability to use it, saved all our lives. You shouldn't have any regrets."

"I do, but I understand what you're saying. I don't want to have to do it again," Chris said.

A train whistle got everyone's attention. Cynthia helped Jeb to his feet, and he went to his dead brother and Boone. Cynthia climbed the steps back to the train platform and motioned for her kids to join her. Chris and Will picked Willie up and carried him into the store, and Jeb and Boone followed.

"What you going to do, Jeb?" Will asked.

"Bury Rupert, and see if I can pay Charlie to sit one of the wagons to Harrisburg. The old fool keeps insisting he can't leave his post, but he's not even in the Army. They'll kill him for sure."

"Maybe he will change his mind," Will said. "We have to see Mrs. Woodberry off and wire her husband she's coming."

"Thank you, Chris, for killing those no goods," Boone said.

"They had it coming," Chris said.

"I'll turn the bodies of those deserters over to the Army when the train gets here," Jeb said. "They can do what they want with them. I'm sure not burying them."

"You might not say who killed them," Chris said. "We don't want to answer a lot of questions, we have to ride on as soon as possible."

"All right, I think I know why but it doesn't matter now. I'll tell them me and my boys did it," Jeb said.

"That would be better," Will said, and they headed for the depot.

"We need to get this over with before someone else shows up and we have to explain ourselves to them," Will said.

"We can try the truth," Chris said.

"Are you crazy? No one's going to believe we came back in time."

"No, not that," Chris said. "I mean, tell them we work for the Flying G. Most people in these parts know about it, and we really do."

"Yeah, we can do that," Will said. The train came into view and started slowing down to a stop next to the depot.

Liddy got up and came over to Chris and Will. "Are you going with us?" she asked.

"No, Liddy," Will said. "You and Gilbert help your mother. Maybe we will see you after the war."

"I'm sorry I said mean things about you. I'm going to miss you," Liddy said.

"That goes for me too," Gilbert said. "We will you too," Chris said. "I know you have heard this before, Gilbert, but remember: a gun is only as good as the man behind it, and the best thing to do is to leave them alone to start with."

"Yes sir," Gilbert said. "Here's your gun," Chris said, and started taking off the holster.

"No, I want you to keep it," Cynthia said and kissed them both on the cheek. "I'll tell my husband how you saved our lives more than once. I want you to have this too," she said, holding out two twenty-dollar gold pieces for Will to take. "I know you need it."

"We can't take that. It's time for you to get on the train. The station master said we have to have an operator on the train to send the telegraph," Will said. "He knows how to get in touch with General Meade's headquarters. What's your husband's first name?"

"Robert," she said.

"Wait here, Chris and I will attend to it. You can buy your tickets."

Chris and Will saw the station master through a window on the train, walking through a packed car of soldiers. He stepped off the train in front of them.

"Where do we find the telegraph operator to send a telegram to Meade's headquarters?" Will asked.

"I'll get him for you, and have him meet you in the station. You better hurry, the train's due out of here in the next fifteen minutes."

"You should reconsider Jeb's offer, Charlie," Chris said. "The Rebs will kill you for sure. You can be of more help by staying alive."

"I wouldn't be if it wasn't for you. Maybe you're right. I'll think about it."

"You do that," Chris said. He and Will went inside the depot and waited. A few minutes later, a boy with rumpled brown hair, steely eyes, and a shuffling gait came in. "The station master said you needed me to send a telegram to General Meade's headquarters," the boy said.

"You're the telegraph operator?" Chris asked.

"I am. I work for the railroad. Name's Thomas Alva Edison, they call me Al."

"You're Thomas Edison?" Will asked.

"Yes, what was the message you wanted sent?"

"How old are you?" Will asked.

"Sixteen. We're wasting time," he said.

"Yes we are," Will said. "The telegram is to Colonel Robert Woodberry at General Meade's headquarters. Send this message: 'Will be arriving with children today by train at 8pm, Cynthia.'"

"Write it down, I don't hear good," Edison said.

Will wrote the message out and handed it to him.

Edison looked at the message and typed it out on the telegraph. "That will be fifty cents. Here's your receipt," he said, and ripped the sheet off the telegraph.

"That lady standing outside will pay you. Would you sign this receipt," Will said.

Edison picked up a pencil, signed his name on the paper, got up, and walked outside to Mrs. Woodberry.

Will looked at Chris and grinned.

"I don't believe what I just saw," Chris said.

"You're just jealous," Will said, and folded the paper and put it in his pocket.

An Army captain appeared on the platform and walked up to Cynthia, he tipped his hat.

Chris and Will were watching the Captain when the station master came in.

"Might be best to stay where you are right now," he said.

"I think you're right," Will said.

"Can I be of service, ma'am?" the captain asked.

"Thank you, Captain, but I think we're okay. We're sending a telegram to my husband to let him know we're coming," she said. The captain glanced at Will and Chris in the depot. "Your husband's in the Army?" he asked.

"Yes. Colonel Robert Woodberry."

"I have met the colonel, a fine officer. Have a pleasant trip," he said, tipped his hat again, and walked back to the train.

The train whistle bellowed, and the conductor leaned out of the train and yelled, "All aboard!"

"Thank goodness for small talk," Will said.

"Yeah," Chris said. They walked out of the depot, and escorted Cynthia and the kids to the train.

"Goodbye," Cynthia said. She hugged them both and dropped two twenty-dollar gold pieces in Will's pocket, without him knowing it.

Cynthia and her children climbed on the train and waved as it pulled out of the station.

Chris and Will stepped off the platform and Jeb walked up. "I decided to not say anything about the deserters," he said. "I put them in a hole behind the store, they didn't deserve a Christian burial. I told Charlie to keep quiet about it too. Their horses didn't have a US brand so I'm keeping them. Boone is getting Rupert ready to bury on that hill over there," he said, pointing at the hill. "We're leaving after we bury him. Best you go now."

"We'll do that, Jeb. We have our reasons for not wanting to deal with the Army, but we're not deserters. I wanted you to know."

"That makes me feel better," Jeb said.

"Good," Will said. They mounted and rode away.

"Well, back to the matter at hand," Chris said.

"If we don't find Kaman, we might try going back to the mountain. Although, I don't think we can get back to our time if we don't do it when he does. It's all a guess anyway. Not every day you become a time traveler."

"Nope," Will said. "I just want to be one, one more time, to get home."

"Time will tell," Chris said.

"You made a funny," Will said.

"I did," Chris said and laughed.

14

It had been three days since Chris and Will disappeared. After a search by ranch hands on horseback, Jim Goodman enlisted the aid of all the local law enforcement agencies. They found the truck and trailer, diggers and fence posts, and some human bones that were too old to be those of Chris and Will. To complicate matters, two of the searchers turned up missing.

Jim was in his truck on his way back to the mountain with Kirby Littlefield, when his cell rang. "That you, Chris?" he asked.

"No," the voice said, "this is Deputy Sheriff Bill Able. We found one of the missing rescue worker's body, something chewed him up pretty bad. There was enough left to identify him, he was a National Guard sergeant. It's not looking good for finding Chris and Will alive."

"Maybe not, but I know Chris. If there's any way to survive, he will find it."

"I hope you're right. I'll let you know what the lab says about the body."

"Thanks," Jim said and hung up. Sully was already at the mountain with a posse, ready to start another day, when Jim and Kirby arrived. Sully walked over to Jim's truck. "We're ready to go when you give the word," he said.

"They found one of the missing men," Jim said. "Something ate part of him."

"Not surprising out here," Sully said. "You go down, something is going to get you.

"I thought of something we haven't checked yet. There was a cave somewhere on this mountain. I don't remember exactly where, it's been so long ago since I was up here, but I know there was one. We've covered every inch of the mountain and I haven't seen the cave. A cave only disappears two ways. It caves in, or the entrance gets covered up; and we didn't see anything to indicate a cave-in."

"You're thinking they could have been in the cave and the entrance got blocked?" Kirby asked.

"Possible, that's the only thing left. If they're not in the cave, I don't think they're on the mountain."

"I would think their cell phones would work in the cave, if they still had them," Jim said, "but maybe not. I've called both a hundred times. We have to find the cave, we're running out of time."

"This whole thing is my fault," Sully said. "I was trying to instill some discipline in them. I should have known better. There have been several people come up here that never came back."

"Hindsight is always 20/20, Sully. Most of the stories about this mountain my great-

grandpa made up to keep people off his land, but something unusual did occur this time, because two strong and smart young men don't just disappear without a trace.

"We'll inform the law enforcement agencies about the cave and fan out across the mountain. Make sure our boys have their rifles in case they run into trouble. Pass the word to everyone to fire two shots if they find the cave."

"Slim has your horses saddled," Sully said.

"Let's do it," Jim said.

"I'll wait to call Pat," Kirby said. "No sense in getting her hopes up until we know."

"That's probably best," Jim said. "Julie will take care of her."

15

The sun was hanging low on the horizon, as Chris and Will rode through a plush green meadow covered with sweet-smelling yellow and blue wildflowers.

"I was thinking, Chris," Will said. "You know, helping that family kind of gives you that warm fuzzy feeling, doesn't it?"

"Yes it does, but if we don't find Kaman, we may get some feelings we don't want."

"What do you miss most?" Will asked.

"The ranch, and my friends," Chris said.

"Me too. I wonder what would happen if I dialed my phone?" Will asked.

"Nothing, dumbass, it's 1863."

"You don't know for sure. We're here from another time, maybe it would go through time."

"And you're a college boy," Chris said, shaking his head.

"I might check it out later, but I won't now because you'll laugh at me."

"I sure will," Chris said. "Can we drop the nonsense and get back to figuring out how to get back to 2013 where your phone will work?"

Will looked at Chris and laughed. "I had you going for a minute, didn't I? You were wondering if it would," Will said.

"Oh, you were playing a joke on me. Or were you?"

"You'll never know," Will said.

In the next instant, a roaring sound streaked across the sky, and the ground came flying up with a crash on the other side of a hill, then another and another. Their horses started rearing up and turning around and around, Chris and Will hanging on. Before the sound died, the roar was going the other way, and crashed into the trees on the other side of the meadow.

"We're in the middle of an artillery barrage," Will said, "let's get out of here."

"Which way?" Chris asked.

"This way!" Will yelled and kicked Rover, and he took off with Spot right behind him. They rode away from the artillery fire and stopped on a hill, in some trees high above the meadow.

A horde of Confederate soldiers on horseback came over the hill, riding like the wind with their leader in front, charging across the meadow. He had a feather stuck in the brim of his black hat, and his sword pointed at the tree line on the other side of the meadow. Seconds later, Union cavalry came riding out from the trees. A man on a big black horse, wearing a white hat and a red neckerchief, was leading the charge. Wildflowers were blowing in every direction as the galloping horses raced through the meadow. The two armies met in the middle, and a fierce battle on horseback began. Soldiers on both sides were dropping like flies. The wildflowers were now yellow, blue, and red from the blood of the soldiers splattered across the meadow. In less than ten minutes, the Confederate ranks were broken by the furious Union charge and they retreated back over the hill, the Union cavalry in hot pursuit.

"It's like watching a movie, but it's real," Chris said.

"There will be more as both armies move closer to Gettysburg," Will said.

"We got to hook up with Kaman tomorrow, somewhere, before he gets to the mountain," Chris said.

They heard hoof beats and saw three Union soldiers break into the open, riding hard toward them.

"What do we do now?" Will asked.

"Stay where you are," Chris said. "We can't outrun a bullet, and I don't want to kill them. We'll have to talk our way out of this."

"From the look on their faces, you better start talking," Will said. "I'm going to stick Edison's receipt in my boot."

"They won't give a hoot about that."

"I know, that's why I'm going to take care of it."

The riders rode up next to Chris and Will. One was a captain and the other two were privates, all three had their rifles pointed at them.

"Get their guns, boys," the captain said.

"Would you look at that, captain," one of the soldiers said. "These two are carrying them fancy repeaters they been telling us about."

"Maybe the Rebs have them now," the captain said.

"No," Chris said, "we bought them. We're cattle buyers from the Flying G. We sell cattle to the Union Army, we're on your side."

"How do I know you're telling the truth? Get off them horses," the captain said.

Will and Chris dismounted and held on to the reins.

"Let's see what you got in your pockets," the captain said. "Empty them out on the ground."

"This should be interesting," Chris said, pitching his cell phone on the ground.

The three soldiers hit the ground.

"What are you doing?" Will asked.

One of the privates grabbed the cell phone, threw it as far as he could, and waited. "Must have been a dud, Captain," he said.

"That's not a grenade, I have one too," Will said and took his phone out of his pocket.

The other soldier slapped the phone out of Will's hand, picked it up, and threw it away. They waited again for something to happen. "I got it, whatever it was," the soldier said.

"That was quick thinking," the captain said. "I may have to recommend you two for a medal. Wait 'til the General hears about them things."

"They weren't dangerous," Will said. "Then what are they?" the captain asked.

"Nothing now. I would tell you, but you still wouldn't know. It didn't work anyway."

"You did try it," Chris said.

"Why not? Nothing else is like it's supposed to be," Will said.

"That's true," Chris said.

"Shut up," the captain said. "Boys, search them, I don't want any more surprises."

The two soldiers removed the rest of their possessions, put them in a bag, and handed it to the captain.

"Did you see what he got out of my pocket?" Will asked.

"No, what?"

"Two twenty-dollar gold pieces. Cynthia must have slipped them in my pocket when we were saying goodbye."

"Nice lady," Chris said. "You won't see those gold pieces again."

"Looks like you got nothing to prove you're from the Flying G," the captain said.

"Guess I'll have to hang you from that big oak over there."

"Captain," one of the privates said, "can we have their horses if you hang them? They are fine looking animals."

"They're quarter horses, they were bred for speed," Chris said.

"What are you doing," Will asked, "encouraging them to hang us?"

"Wait," Chris said, "I have a receipt in my saddle bags for some cattle we sold to the government. Can I get it?"

"Go ahead," the captain said, "real slow-like."

Chris reached in his saddle bags and felt around, and came out with a piece of paper. "Here," he said, "this is a receipt for fifty head last month." He handed the receipt to the captain, the captain looked at the receipt.

"This says you sold fifty head to the federal government with FDA approval on May 5, 2013," he said. "Shouldn't there be a year? And what is FDA?"

They both stood there, staring at each other, then Will spoke. "That was the time," he said. "You know, military time, 2013, thirteen minutes after eight. And FDA was the inspector's initials."

"You're smarter than you look," Chris said.

"Something still ain't right here, but maybe you better have a talk with the General before we hang you," the captain said. "Tie their hands and put them on their horses. We'll see what the General wants to do with them."

"Looks like your plan's not working, Chris," Will said. "We better go to Plan B, if we can think of one."

16

The soldiers led them down the hill to the meadow. Hundreds of soldiers lay dead and wounded in the late afternoon sun. Both sides were trying to remove their comrades from the battlefield during a lull in the fighting. A horde of hungry buzzards circled overhead.

The two soldiers stopped beside a wagon inside the tree line, and dismounted next to a tent with a sign that read 'Commanding Officer.'

The captain rode up. "Bain, tie them to the wagon and stay with them. Seaton, you can go back to your squad, I'm going to tell the General," he said, and tied his horse on the picket line next to Rover and Spot.

"Your name is Bain?" Chris asked.

"Yeah," he said, "what's it to you?"

"That's my name," Chris said, "Christopher Bain."

"We ain't any kin, Reb," he said. "All my folk are from around here."

"Well, I'll be," Will said. "You do kind of favor."

"What are you doing, Will?" Chris asked.

"I'm working on Plan B."

A slim young man with blonde hair, wearing a brigadier general's uniform with a red neckerchief, emerged from the tent. He walked over to the wagon and looked down at Chris and Will.

"You spies for the Confederacy?" he asked.

"No," Will Said. "I'm William Littlefield, and this is Christopher Bain. We're on your side."

"Where did you get the repeaters and the hand grenades?" he asked. "That something the Rebs have now?"

"They weren't hand grenades. They have nothing to do with war," Will said. "What kind of force will I be facing tomorrow?"

"We have no idea, General. Like I told you, we're on your side."

"Never saw any federal money like you had in your pockets before, and the cards with your pictures on them said you was drivers. That mean you're mule skinners?"

"No, we're from the Flying G Ranch," Chris said.

"Captain," he said, "send a runner to General Meade's headquarters and tell him we captured two Reb spies with repeating rifles like I have never seen before. Would he like to question them some more before we hang them? I'll keep the rifles for now."

"Yes sir," the captain said, saluted, and hurried away.

"We're not spies," Will said. "We're trying to get back to the ranch. Didn't the captain give you the receipt we had for the cattle?"

"You could have got that anywhere," he said.

"You ever hear of a Gatling gun, General?" Will asked.

"I've heard of it. Some new-fangled thing that will probably jam every time you use it. No gun can shoot that fast without burning up the barrel, and it would slow me down anyway."

"You might rethink that one, General Custer," Chris said.

"I don't think so," he said. "How do you know my name?"

"Everyone knows about you," Will said. "Congratulations on your recent promotion to general, you're the youngest ever. The next three days will be your finest hours."

"Every hour is my finest hour."

"For a while," Chris said.

"I don't have time to fool with the likes of you two anymore, I have a war to win."

"Yes you do, General, and you will," Will said. "You didn't get near enough credit."

Custer tilted his head and stroked his mustache a couple of strokes as he eyed the two men. "I don't know if you're being complimentary or sarcastic, but either way, you're going to hang," he said and walked back to his tent.

"You two stay right where you are," Bain said. "You give me any troubles, he won't have to hang you, I'll shoot you both." Bain sat down out of reach against a big tree, and laid his rifle across his lap.

"If you did shoot us, you might be shooting one of your family members," Will said.

"He ain't none of my kin. He would be in the Army like me, fighting for the Union," Bain said.

"I think I know what you're doing," Chris said. "But that's not going to work either."

Will whispered to Chris, "Just follow my lead."

"I was thinking, Private Bain," Will said, "if they hang Chris and you find out he is one of your kin, it would be a sad day. Chris was born and raised around here, too, maybe
he's a cousin."

"I know what you're doing, mister, and it won't work," Bain said.

"Told you," Chris said.

"The war won't last forever," Will said. "I would hate to be in your shoes when you have to answer for killing one of your own."

"Knock it off and stay put, it's getting dark and I need some rest," he said, and pulled his hat down over his eyes.

"You should think it over, Bain, before you do something you will regret," Will said.

"You're wasting your breath," Chris said, "he's asleep. Like most everyone else is, except the sentries. I think the time for talking is over. We got to get out of these ropes and start tracking Kaman. If we don't go tonight, we may not get another chance."

"We could change a lot of history if we wanted to," Will said. "For example, what if we told Custer what was going to happen to him?"

"We have no right to do that," Chris said.

"I guess you're right. I don't think he would believe us anyway," Will said. "They made the wrong Custer a general. Thomas won a medal of honor in May, and will win another before the war is over, and he's barely a footnote at Little Big Horn."

"You keep wandering off to Never Never Land with your wild stories and you won't be nothing," Chris said. "This is our best chance to escape. We got to get our mind on getting out of here tonight, or we'll be hanging from a rope tomorrow."

"The knife! I just remembered," Will said. "You tied the scabbard on the saddle, I stuck it under the saddle horn. I think it's still there, but Rover is tied to the picket line, we're out of luck."

"Not yet...if I don't wake up Bain. Rover, come here," Chris said. The horse looked at him.

"Rover, come here," he said again, in a sterner voice. The horse pulled on the reins and they came loose from the rope. Rover walked over next to Chris and stood there.

"I see the strap. Good thing they keep their horses saddled in a combat area," Chris said. "If we can get it, we can cut ourselves loose."

"That sentry is going to be back this way soon," Will said.

Chris struggled to stand with the rope on his ankles and leaned against Rover. "Turn around, Will, with your back to Rover," Chris said. "I'll lift you up, you get the knife and start sawing on those ropes."

Will turned around and Chris lifted him up on his shoulders. Will retrieved the knife and started sawing on the ropes. They soon gave way, and he finished untying himself and then Chris. Bain was snoring like a bull elephant.

"Don't wake Bain," Chris said.

The Colt and holster was hanging on Spot's saddle horn. "That was a mistake, Private Bain," Chris thought, as he strapped the holster on. "I'm going to get the rifles from Custer's tent," Chris said.

"Are you crazy? We don't have time for that. Custer will probably wake up, and then we're dead for sure."

"We need those rifles," Chris said.

Chris made his way to Custer's tent. The flap was open, and Custer was in bed. He stepped inside the tent and saw the rifles leaning against a small portable table. He picked them up, and Custer groaned and turned over. He froze and almost peed his pants. When Custer didn't wake up, Chris took a big breath, hurried out of the tent with the rifles, and caught up with Will.

"Here," he said, handing Will a rifle, "let's get out of here."

They walked their horses beside sleeping soldiers, to a small creek on the edge of the encampment.

"Better let the horses get a drink, we got a hard ride," Chris said.

"Man, I was thinking about jumping in," Will said. "We been wearing the same clothes for almost a week."

"It won't matter how you smell when you're dead."

"I didn't say it would," Will said.

"If they come after us, don't stop for anything until they give up the chase," Chris said. "If we don't make it, it's been nice knowing you, Will."

"You too, Chris. Good luck."

"We're going to need it," Chris said.

"I think we're about to find out how fast these quarter horses of your's are."

"I think so," Chris said.

"Don't move," a voice said from behind them.

They turned around, and Private Bain was standing a few feet away, with his rifle pointed at them.

"You're supposed to be sleeping," Will said.

"Take that Colt off, and both of you, back away from them horses," Bain said.

Chris unbuckled the holster and let it fall to the ground, and then they took a step back from the horses.

"We're not spies, Bain," Will said. "Why don't you look the other way and let us get out of here?"

"I'm no traitor. Put your hands on your head and start walking back to the wagon," he said.

Chris and Will started walking, and Bain picked up the reins of the horses, the Colt, and followed. They walked back to the wagon and a sentry showed up with his rifle pointed at them.

"Keep your rifle on them, Seaton, while I tie them back up," Bain said.

"Good thing you found them, Bain," Seaton said. "You know what the rules are. They escape, they hang you."

"Yeah I know, how about you don't say anything," Bain said, as he tied the horses to the picket line.

"Okay with me," Seaton said. "Best you don't wake the General."

"You really are making a mistake," Will said.

"You sure are," Chris said.

"Shut up," Bain said. "I ain't going to let you out of my sight again until you're dangling from a rope."

Bain took the rifles out of the saddle scabbards and placed them and the Colt back in Custer's tent.

"It's going to be light soon," Bain said, "you better start making peace with your maker. The General ain't going to wait long to hang you once the sun comes up."

"What's your given name, Bain?" Will asked.

"None of your business," Bain said.

"Don't you want to know if you're hanging your kin?" Will asked.

"No," he said.

"You've already tried that," Chris said.

"I know… I couldn't think of anything else. Looks like this is it."

"I'm afraid so," Chris said. "We almost got away."

"Almost don't count," Bain said and grinned.

"Yeah, too bad," Chris said.

"Thanks, Seaton, for your help," Bain said. "I think I can handle it from here." Seaton nodded and walked away.

17

The morning light was working its way through a heavy fog, covering the still-sleeping Union troops when Custer came out of his tent, wearing his white Stetson and red neckerchief, his hand on his battle sword. He stopped, looked across the meadow, and listened, as the sounds of Confederate movement became louder.

"Looks like they're getting ready for round two," he said, to no one in particular. "I'm going to wipe 'em out this time."

"What do you want me to do with the prisoners, General?" Bain asked.

"I don't think we're going to have time for a hanging party, and I haven't heard from General Meade. Form a firing squad. Dig a hole and shoot them."

"Yes sir," Bain said.

Seaton came walking by. "Hey Seaton," Bain said, "the General said for me to form a firing squad to execute the prisoners. Go get me two more men, we need four. I'll stay with the prisoners. We'll do it right here."

A colonel, two majors, and four captains walked up beside Custer.

"Good morning, gentleman," Custer said. "The staff meeting is going to be short this morning. It looks like the fight is on again, tell your men to prepare themselves. I figure we got less than an hour before all hell breaks loose. Any man caught not doing his duty

will be shot for cowardice. Now get to your post. Good luck."

The officers scattered in all different directions. Custer's aide led his black stallion to him. Custer looked at Chris and Will. "May god have mercy on your souls," he said, placed his foot in the stirrup, and mounted.

"You're making a big mistake, General," Chris said. "We're not spies."

"I don't make mistakes," Custer said.

"This is just one of many," Will said. "Unfortunately, you got more guts than brains."

"If they don't get the firing squad together soon, I'll shoot you myself," Custer said.

"They're coming, General," Bain said.

Seaton and two other men walked up. "We're here for the firing squad," Seaton said. Bain went to get Chris and Will.

Three riders galloped up. One was a colonel, and the other two sergeants. The colonel and the sergeants rode up beside Custer and saluted. Custer returned their salute.

"Good morning, General," the colonel said. "I hear you have some spies. General Meade thought it would be good to interrogate them some more. I brought Sergeant Atkinson and Sergeant Major Hawkins with me to help out."

The three men looked like characters out of a John Wayne movie. The colonel sat tall in the saddle, wearing a sweat-stained hat. He had deep blue eyes, gray sideburns, and a short black mustache. The sergeant major was a stout-looking man with a rugged, weather-worn face, broad shoulders, and large hands; maybe a blacksmith in civilian life. Atkinson looked more like a professor than a soldier, with a slim build, droopy eyes, and a beard. They all looked tired.

"They're right there, Colonel Woodberry," Custer said and pointed at Chris and Will. "I was about to execute them."

Chris and Will looked at each other.

"Excuse me, Colonel," Chris said, "would you be Colonel Robert Woodberry?"

"Yes," he said.

"Boy, are we glad to see you. We know your wife, Cynthia, and your kids, Gilbert and Liddy. We saved them from an ambush and put them on a train."

"Are you Chris and Will?" Colonel Woodberry asked.

"Yes we are," Chris said.

"These men aren't spies, General. They saved my family's life and sent them to me."

"That don't mean they're not spies. May have been a cover-up to conceal their true identity," Custer said.

"I don't think so. Cynthia said they worked for the Flying G Ranch, and Old Man

Goodman is a strong supporter of the Union."

"Well, you can have them. You might let General Meade look at the repeaters they had, they're in my tent."

"I'll do that," Colonel Woodberry said. "General Meade wants you to move closer to Gettysburg, to cover the rear of his troops along with the 2nd Maine Regiment. Lee is positioning his army to make an attack from the front and rear, somewhere around Gettysburg in the next day or two, and you have to prevent a breakthrough at all cost. He also told me to tell you what a fine job you're doing, and to keep it up."

"I intend to, Colonel. Give the General my best." He took one last look at Chris and Will. "I'd keep a close eye on those two if I was you, Colonel. There's something not right about them. Take Bain with you for a little extra security," he said and rode away.

"Untie them, Private," Colonel Woodberry said to Bain.

"Yes sir," Bain said and untied them. "You want their papers and guns?"

"Give them back to them," Woodberry said.

"Pardon, sir, you going to give them the rifles back?"

"Yes."

"Yes sir," Bain said, "but I don't think the General will be too happy about that."

"Don't worry about it, Private," Woodberry said. "They're my responsibility, not yours."

Bain got the weapons and handed them to Chris and Will. Chris strapped on the Colt and they walked over to their horses, put their rifles in the scabbards, untied them, and climbed up in the saddle. Bain untied his horse and joined them.

"Colonel," Will said, "I had two twenty-dollar gold pieces they took from me. I would like them back."

"You got them, Bain?" the colonel asked.

"Yes sir," Bain said, and dug them out of his pocket and handed them to Will.

"I could have you court-martialed for that," the colonel said to Bain.

"I forgot. I thought we were going to hang them," Bain said.

"Sure you did," Will said.

Colonel Woodberry looked at the gun on Chris's hip. "My wife said you was quite a marksman with that Colt."

"It's really your gun," Chris said. "You can have it back."

"No, you keep it, I got one. You boys can ride along with us if you want to," Woodberry said, "the place is crawling with Confederates."

"Are you going to Gettysburg?" Will asked.

"Yes we are. General Meade is on the move there as we speak."

"Thanks, we'll take you up on that," Chris said.

"We'll take a small detour north to avoid the Rebs, then turn east on the other side of Kickapoo Creek," Colonel Woodberry said.

"How long will it take to get there, Colonel?" Chris said.

"If we don't run in to any Rebs, about two hours," he said.

18

The six riders were about a mile away from Custer's camp when they heard artillery fire.

"Looks like Custer's got company," Woodberry said. "Keep moving and look out for Rebel scouts. Bain, take the point."

"Yes sir," Bain said, spurred his horse, rode out in front of them, and disappeared around a bend in the trail.

They rode along in silence through the dense forests, down a hill, with only the sounds of war echoing through the trees. Even the birds knew to be quiet.

Without warning, a shot rang out and Sergeant Atkinson tumbled off the back of his horse and hit the ground, dead. A bullet hit a tree inches from the sergeant majors head.

"Dismount and find cover," Woodberry said.

They grabbed their rifles and hit the ground.

Bain appeared, riding as fast as his horse could go. Bullets whizzed by him, clipping braches off nearby trees.

"They're on the ridge above us," he yelled, as his horse came to a stop and he dropped off and rolled over on the ground in the high grass next to Chris.

"This your doing, Reb?" Bain asked Chris.

"You won't give it up, will you," Chris said.

"I don't see anyone," Will said.

"They're there, I saw the muzzle blast," Bain said.

"How many?" Will asked.

"Don't know," Bain said.

"Stay down and let them come to us," Colonel Woodberry said.

They lay on the ground in the grass, waiting.

"Shouldn't we try to ride out of here, Colonel?" Chris asked.

"No," Colonel Woodberry said, "that's what they want us to do so they can pick us off. Sergeant Major, see if you and Will can get to that knoll over there without being seen, that high grass will give you some cover. We'll have them in a crossfire with the repeaters when they come down the ridge."

"Yes sir," Hawkins said. "Follow me, Will. Stay as close to the ground as you can."

"I'm right behind you," Will said.

The two men hugged the ground as they crawled through the high grass, with their rifles to a knoll, and slid off into a narrow ditch.

"They're there," Woodberry said. "We wait them out."

An hour passed before the sound of rustling leaves broke the silence.

Colonel Woodberry raised his hand slightly and pointed in the direction the sound came from. Bain and Chris nodded. The chilling sound of Rebel yells followed, as five Confederate soldiers charged down the ridge, screaming.

"Now," Colonel Woodberry said, and they jumped up and fired. Four of the five went down from the rapid fire from both directions. The remaining soldier was charging Bain with his bayonet. Bain fired and missed.

Chris drew the Colt and fired, the soldier dropped his rifle and collapsed to the ground beside Bain, his blood splattering across Bain's boots.

Bain looked at Chris and gave out a big sigh of relief.

Three more soldiers came charging down the ridge behind Will and the sergeant major. "Look out!" Chris yelled. Will and the sergeant major turned and fired, and two of the soldiers went down. The other one made a quick exit behind some trees and disappeared.

"Let's get out of here," Woodberry said. They ran down the hill and saw Spot standing under a tree at the foot of the hill. "Come here, Spot," Chris said and the horse came to him. He got on the horse.

"Climb aboard, Will," he said and reached out for Will's hand. "Rover won't be too far away."

They found Rover and the other four horses together on the other side of the creek and brought them back.

The colonel, Bain and the sergeant major were crouched down behind some trees, looking up the hill where the Confederates came from.

They all got on their horses, the sergeant major tied Atkinson's body across Atkinson's horse's saddle, and they rode away at a hard gallop. A short time later, Colonel Woodberry gave the signal to slow down and they slowed their horses to a walk.

Will rode up beside Chris. "Well, looks like we're in the war whether we want to or not," Will said.

"I was hoping we wouldn't have to kill anyone, but it was like you said, them or us."

"We're not there yet," Will said. "There may be more."

"I was thinking about that," Chris said.

Bain stopped his horse and waited for Chris and Will to catch up. "The name's Terry," he said. "I was wrong, sorry."

Chris nodded, "I'll remember that."

"Thanks for saving my life," Bain said, "maybe we are related."

"I doubt it. That was Will trying to keep from getting hanged."

Bain smiled. "Just the same, it would be alright with me if we were," he said.

"Me too," Chris said.

They rode into the Union camp, where thousands of men were spread out across the pastures and rocks, preparing for battle.

Colonel Woodberry stopped in front of a small house with officers going in and out. "Stay here, boys, I have to tell General Meade what happened. He may want to talk to you." He dropped down off his horse and went in the house.

"We may have got ourselves into something we can't get out of," Will said. "The Battle of Gettysburg was the most costly battle in the history of American warfare. More men died in three days than all of the ten-year war in Vietnam. At this point, I think we might as well prepare ourselves to live out our life in the eighteen-hundreds… if we don't get killed first."

Colonel Woodberry came to the door and motioned for Will and Chris to join him. "Bring your rifles," he said.

"Looks like we're going to meet the man," Will said. "He's making his headquarters in the widow Leister's house."

"Where is she?" Chris asked.

"How would I know," Will said.

"You act like you know everything else," Chris said.

"I know he could have ended the war right here and now, if he had chased Lee into Virginia."

"Keep your history mouth to yourself when we go in," Chris said.

Chris and Will walked over to Colonel Woodberry with their rifles in hand.

"The General wants to meet you and have a look at those rifles," Woodberry said.

They walked in the house. General Meade was sitting on a folding chair next to a table, his pistol belt and hat laying on the table. He stood up and looked at Chris and Will.

"Gentleman, Colonel Woodberry told me about you saving his family and those repeaters. How did you come by them?"

"We got them from the Flying G, we work there," Chris said. "We're trying to get home."

"I see, you mind if I take a look?"

"No sir, of course not," Will said and handed the General his rifle.

Meade looked it over. "This is something new," he said. "I didn't know Winchester had a repeater. I've seen some Spencer rifles, but nothing like this. Do you know where Goodman got them?" Meade asked.

Chris looked at Will, not knowing what to say.

"I think he acquired them from Winchester for testing, they haven't come out yet," Will said.

"I didn't think so. This rifle will revolutionize warfare. Might have known the Army would be the last to know. If they do make them available during the war, Grant will get them first. He's got his eye on the presidency if we win this war, and he'll do whatever it takes to make himself look good."

General Meade sat back down and looked up at Chris and Will. "Sorry, didn't mean to get into politics. We can use you and your rifles, but I won't demand it. You're not in the Army, the decision is yours. Thank you for helping my men get out of a jam."

"You're welcome, sir," Will said.

"Colonel, see to it that they get something to eat and make out a pass for them to get through the lines and I'll sign it, if that's what they want to do," General Meade said.

"Thank you, sir, we appreciate it," Chris said.

"I'm sure you will be victorious, General," Will said.

General Meade nodded and they walked out of the house. "The chuck wagon is in front of you, I'll get you the passes," Colonel Woodberry said.

"Thank you, Colonel," Will said.

"Wait here," he said and walked away.

"He seems to be disappointed," Will said.

"I understand," Chris said, "but we don't belong here. Whatever we do won't change anything."

"We may have to think about that," Will said.

19

"Pass me the syrup," Will said. "These biscuits are so hard, they need a little help going down. Boy, what I wouldn't give for a McDonalds."

"You better be glad to get them."

"I am, but that doesn't mean I have to like 'em," Will said. "Eat them, we got a long ride and nothing else to eat."

"Do you really think we will find Kaman in all this humanity?"

"No, but we have to try," Chris said.

"Why? Maybe we should give it up and stick around. Besides, I don't look forward to having to deal with a bunch of zombies. They give me the creeps just thinking about them. We don't know how many there are, we may wind up being one. This might be the less of the two evils."

"You're the Civil War expert. Do you know what the odds are for us to survive this battle?"

"Yeah, slim to none," Will said.

"And you like those odds better than trying to find Kaman and taking our chances with the zombies?"

"Yes," Will said. "You can stay if you want to, I'm going to find Kaman and go home. We may not have to deal with the zombies," Chris said.

"You're the one that said we would have to wait until Kaman became a zombie."

"No, I said we would have to be there when he got there."

"That's not what you said, you're just trying to convince me to go with you."

"You do whatever you want to, I'm going home. If that don't work, I'll figure out something else."

"I think I'm going to tell the colonel I'll stay," Will said.

"Suit yourself."

Colonel Woodberry showed up with the passes signed by General Meade and gave them to Chris and Will. "You should ride out of here as soon as you can," he said.

"Thank you, Colonel, good luck," Chris said.

"Colonel, I'm thinking about staying," Will said.

"I wanted you to," Woodberry said, "but after thinking about it, that may not be a good idea. Surviving the war is one thing, but one of our own would kill you for that rifle for their own survival."

"Never thought about that," Will said.

"You still want to stay?" Chris asked.

"Maybe not, thanks Colonel for the advice."

Colonel Woodberry shook hands with them. "I'll say hello to Cynthia and the kids for you," he said and walked away.

"Looks like I don't have a choice," Will said. "Dammed if you do, dammed if you don't."

"That's about the size of it," Chris said. "We'll saddle the horses after we eat and head for Seven Stars."

"I'm done trying to eat these biscuits, it's like trying to eat a rock."

"You're going to get hungry," Chris said.

"Not that hungry."

"Okay, I'm not giving you any of mine"

"Tell you what; to please you, I'll use them for a cushion, that saddle gets hard," Will said. "I'll put one in each back pocket, that's about all they're good for." Will stuck a biscuit in each back pocket and patted his butt.

"Be a wise ass, you're not hurting me. You weren't really thinking about staying were you?" Chris asked. "You were just pulling my chain, like now, with the biscuits, right?"

"Nope. I was serious, but I'm going now."

"That's more like it, let's get ready," Chris said.

Will and Chris were saddling their horses when Private Bain rode up. "The Colonel said you was leaving, going back to the ranch."

"That's right," Chris said, "I was going to say goodbye."

"I thought maybe you could deliver a letter to my wife for me. Her name's Barbara Ann, she's in Morganville. That's not too far from the Flying G." Chris looked at Will. "Take the letter," Will said.

"Okay, I know where it is, I'll see what I can do," Chris said.

"Thanks, Chris," Bain said and handed him the letter. "Maybe we can get together after the war."

"Yeah, maybe so," Chris said.

"See you," he said, turned his horse around, and rode away.

"I won't be able to deliver this letter," Chris said.

"He doesn't know that, and there's a good chance he never will, but it was the right thing to do. You do favor, same hair and eyes."

Chris smiled. "I hope he makes it," he said.

"Yeah, I hope we all do," Will said.

20

Chris and Will rode out of General Meade's headquarters, headed for Seven Stars. Thousands of Union soldiers were converging on Gettysburg to prepare for the arrival of Lee's Army. It seemed like they would never stop coming.

"Unbelievable," Will said, "I thought I could visualize the magnitude of this battle, but I think the only way to really know is to have been here when it happened."

"I know what you're thinking, but we won't make any difference by staying. History has already made its decision and it was the right one," Chris said.

A colonel rode up to Chris and Will. "What are you men doing here? Why aren't you in uniform?" he asked.

"We're not soldiers," Chris said. "We're on our way home to the Flying G Ranch. We have a pass from General Meade."

"Let's see it," he said.

Chris took the paper out of his pocket and handed it to the colonel. "You have one too?" he asked, looking at Will, and handed the pass back to Chris.

"Yes sir," Will said.

Before Will could get the pass out of his pocket, a sergeant ran up to the colonel. "Colonel Littlefield, the Rebs have broken through at C Company," the sergeant said.

"Get word to Captain Benson to hold his ground," Colonel Littlefield said. "I'll get help. We have to slow down their advance to Gettysburg."

"Yes sir," the sergeant said and hurried away.

"Forget the pass; both of you get out of here, now," Littlefield said. He turned his horse around and rode away as fast as he could.

"That was him," Will said. "That was my great-grandpa."

"You said you wanted to meet him," Chris said.

"Yes, but not like that. I wanted to talk to him."

"I don't think that's going to happen. Let's ride while we still can."

They took off at a gallop, weaving their way through the advancing troops, when a Confederate artillery round flew over their heads and landed not too far away, killing several soldiers and injuring more. Before they could find cover, another round landed even closer. Several pieces of shrapnel peppered Rover, cutting one of his reins. He reared up, and took off across a field with hundreds of soldiers that were running away from the artillery fire. Will hung on, trying to get control of him, as they disappeared into the trees on the other side of the field. Chris started after Will, but was blocked by all the soldiers running past him. A few seconds later, Union artillery was answering the Confederacy. He rode behind a big rock and hung on to Spot. After about thirty minutes of deafening horror from the artillery blast, it stopped, and screams of agony from the dying and wounded took its place again.

In the distance, Chris could hear the yells of Rebel soldiers as they charged the Union lines. So many rifles were firing it sounded like the bowels of hell had opened up. Thick gun smoke floated across the field and disappeared into no man's land. Will and Rover were nowhere in sight.

If he didn't find him by tomorrow morning when the real battle began, there may not be a way out. They would die here and no one would know what happened to them.

Will had become the brother he never had. What started as a way to get Will's dad to help him join the rodeo had turned into a lasting friendship. Kaman might be on his way to the mountain before he found Will, if he ever did, but there was no way he would leave him behind, dead or alive. If it was to end like this, he hoped he could find him and they could go out together. Riding wild horses didn't seem important anymore.

He rode Spot across the field and up a hill, where he had a view of the surrounding terrain. On the other side of the hill he saw Rover, standing at the foot of the hill next to a tree. Chris took a deep breath and rode down the hill expecting to find Will dead, but he wasn't there.

He checked Rover and found some minor cuts from the artillery fire, but nothing serious. The Winchester was still in the scabbard. He took his calf rope out of his saddle bags, tied the rope to the bridle bit for a rein, and led Rover away. If he didn't find Will soon, he may never find him.

21

Chris rode back up the hill with Rover in tow, visually surveying the surrounding area again. There was blood on the grass in different spots, where soldiers had fallen. He saw a crow eating something on the ground and hoped it wasn't a body part. He rode up to the crow and it flew away. He looked on the ground and saw a piece of bread. A little further away was another piece of bread. He lined up the pieces of bread and rode in the same direction, and saw another piece that looked like the outer crust of a biscuit. A big smile came on his face.

"So that's it, you're alive and someone is forcing you to go where you don't want to go. I told you that biscuit would come in handy," he said to himself.

He tied Rover to a tree and kept moving in the same direction, until he heard voices. He tied Spot to a limb, drew the Colt, and sneaked up behind a tree.

Two Confederate soldiers were sitting on a log eating cornbread. One was a tall thin sergeant, with a beard and shoulder-length dirty brown hair. The other one was a lot smaller, no stripes, with a baby face and blonde hair; their rifles were propped against a log. Will was lying on the ground between them, with his hands tied behind his back and a neckerchief stuffed in his mouth.

"We take this Yankee back, I bet we get a promotion," the sergeant said.

"He ain't no soldier," the private said. "Major Johnson said we was supposed to catch a soldier, not a Yankee civilian. Besides, he was knocked out when we found him, all we did was tie his hands."

"We ain't going to tell them that, stupid. He had this paper in his pocket," the sergeant said and shook the paper at the young soldier.

"I can read. It says it's a pass to get through the Yankee lines, so that makes him a blue belly."

"It sure does. We better get going," the sergeant said. "On your feet, Yankee," the private said, and pulled Will up by his arm.

Before they could pick up their rifles from the log, Chris stepped out in the open. "Don't reach for those rifles or I'll have to blow you away," he said.

They looked surprised and the private raised his hands, but the sergeant didn't. "You think you can kill both of us before one of us gets a rifle?" the sergeant asked.

"I know I can. Now, back away and I'll let you walk away from here…as soon as you untie my friend," Chris said.

"Since when?" the private asked. "The Yankees burned down my house in '62 and made me an orphan, raped and killed my sister," the private said.

"I'm sorry that happened, but we didn't have anything to do with it. Untie him," Chris said, "or I'll change my mind."

The private bent down and untied Will. Will got to his feet and pulled the neckerchief out of his mouth. "What took you so long?" he asked ,and grabbed his Meade pass out of the sergeant's hand.

"How did you know I would know what those bread crumbs meant?" Chris asked.

"I didn't, but I knew you were a smart dude, and you were so fond of those biscuits, you would recognize them and come looking for me and figure it out. I got knocked out by a low tree limb when I was trying to corral Rover and when I woke up, these two had me tied up."

"You're full of it. What if the crows had eaten all of the biscuits before I got here?"

"Then we wouldn't be having this conversation."

"There was one chance in a million that would work," Chris said. "If I hadn't seen the crow I would have never seen the bread. If we do get back, remind me to take you to Vegas."

The sergeant lunged for his rifle and Chris fired. The gun stock splintered, and fell off the rifle.

"Damn it, I told you not to do that," he said. He looked at the private. "Don't you try that. How old are you boy?" he asked.

"Fourteen," the private said.

"You're too young to be a soldier," Will said.

Chris and Will heard a noise behind them and turned around. Colonel Littlefield was riding toward them, pistol drawn.

"What are you two still doing here?" he asked, as he reined his horse to a stop.

"These two Rebs were going to take me back to their camp when Chris showed up," Will said.

"You got you two prisoners, Colonel," Chris said. "I didn't want to kill them."

"Well I do," he said. "We're not taking any prisoners."

A shot from the colonel's pistol busted the sergeant's skull. He fell to the ground with what was left of his head, covered in blood. The young soldier took off running. Littlefield put two bullets in his back and he dropped to his knees, gasped, and fell over on the ground.

"Good thing I heard the shot. Now ride and don't come back," Colonel Littlefield said.

"I don't think I like your grandpa very much, Will," Chris said.

"What was that?" Littlefield asked.

"You wouldn't understand, Colonel," Will said. "I don't think I like you either."

"You two ain't making any sense," he said.

"I think you're right, Chris," Will said, "we don't belong here. Let's go home."

"Hop on, I got your horse tied to a tree back up the trail."

Will pulled himself up on Spot, behind Chris. "That boy was only fourteen years old," Chris said. "There was really no need to kill them."

"They were wearing the wrong uniform. War is war," Littlefield said and rode away.

The smell of decaying flesh blew across the hill top.

"Can you believe what just happened?" Chris asked.

"Yeah, I can smell death everywhere," Will said.

22

"If we can get to Seven Stars by tonight, we will be in a position to intercept Kaman tomorrow…if he was telling the truth," Chris said.

"Then what?" Will asked. "Do we try to join him, follow him, or what?"

"I haven't figured that out yet."

"Don't you think it's about time?"

"I'll let you work on that," Chris said.

"You know, it's not like we know what the guy looked like a hundred and fifty years ago," Will said.

"I think we will recognize him. If we don't, we'll ask."

Will stared at Chris. "I didn't think of that. Maybe get a sign like they do at the airports, with his name on it, and walk around yelling 'Kaman!' until he jumps up and shoots our ass, thinking we are trying to get his gold."

"Sometimes you can be a real pain," Chris said. "I don't plan on doing anything stupid, and I hope you don't. We'll let history take its course and go from there."

"Whatever," Will said. "I hate to leave the Rebs without burying them, but we got no way to do it. Maybe their friends will find them before the buzzards do."

"Maybe so. I feel sorry for the kid, he had no business being here."

"Me too, but my grandpa was right about one thing: war is war, and they would have killed us all if they had the chance."

"Won't do any good to think about it now," Chris said. "I saw a creek on the other side of the hill. I think we should stop and get that quick bath you been wanting, and cool off in this heat. We got a hard ride ahead and no biscuits."

"Very funny," Will said.

They rode over the hill to the creek, tied Spot and Rover to a tree, laid their saddle bags, hats, rifles, and the Colt at the edge of the creek bed, and took off their boots. Chris put his Meade pass in his boot. Will checked to make sure the Edison receipt was still in his boot, put the Meade pass in the boot with it, and they jumped in, clothes and all.

After about ten minutes in the water they got out, pitched their saddle bag on the ground, and rode their horses into the creek. They got off and soaked them down, climbed back on, and rode them up on the bank.

"Boy, does that feel good," Will said.

"I feel like I been baptized," Chris said.

"I don't think there's anything holy about us, but we might consider saying a little prayer if we hope to get home. This is a different world with different rules."

"I been thinking about that," Chris said. "The only law here is the law of survival.

They shoot and ask questions later."

"That's for sure," Will said. "We can't flinch if we expect to make it out of here alive."

"I hope you haven't lost those twenty-dollar gold pieces," Chris said. "We may need them for food, for us and the horses."

"I got them," Will said. "Eating may be the least of our worries. If we were in uniform we would have the protection of one side, but we're targets for both sides in civilian clothes."

"That's why I need someone like you with me. I figure with your luck, we're bulletproof," Chris said.

"I won't test it," Will said. "We better hang on to those passes General Meade gave us and stay close to the Union lines."

They hung their saddle bags back on their horses and picked up their gear. "You know I wouldn't have left you behind, dead or alive," Chris said. "I know. That goes for me too. It's a miracle we're still alive."

They heard horses running and several riders topped the hill, headed their way.

"They're wearing the wrong uniforms, with rifles in their hands," Will said. "They must have found their friends."

Chris jumped up on Spot. "I don't think they want to talk about it," he said.

"I think you're right, kemo sabe," Will said, as he grabbed the saddle horn and swung himself up on Rover.

23

Jim poured himself a cup of coffee, and one for Kirby, from his thermos and gazed across the mountain. Low morning clouds circled the top of the mountain like a smoky halo. No one had found the cave, and it was probably too late now if they did.

They sat down on the tailgate of Jim's truck and drank their coffee.

Sully walked up. "I sent Cookie to town to get us all some breakfast," he said. "I think his feelings was hurt because I didn't let him fix it."

"We won't tell him why," Jim said and smiled. Kirby nodded, raised his cup to his lips, and took a sip.

Jim sat his cup on the tailgate and took another look across the mountain. "This is a sad day, Kirby. I loved that boy like my own, and that other kid was a real nice boy."

"Yeah, I know how you feel," Kirby said.

"After we eat," Jim said, "let's saddle up for one more run before we hang it up. There's not much else we can do."

"Boss, there really is a cave in this mountain," Sully said, "I've seen it. Why we can't find it puzzles me."

"So far the only thing we've done is lose two men," Jim said. "One of which, we still can't find. We came looking for two and lost two more. If we don't get off this mountain soon we may lose more. There's something out there that not only kills people, it eats them. I'm afraid that's what happened to Chris and Will."

"What about the horses?" Sully asked.

"They may have run off, or that something got them too. I don't want anyone coming up here again."

"There's a horrible evil on this mountain," Kirby said.

"If they're not in the cave, it must be human, because we haven't found the rifles or any of the other hardware. Only humans would want that," Sully said.

"Up to now I was thinking accident or animals, but you may be right. Someone may have killed them, took their possessions, and left them for the animals; or we have a mad man out there that I have heard stories about before."

"I think everyone around here has. Maybe they're true," Sully said.

"I'll see if the coroner can take a saliva test on the body and find out if it's human or animal. That way we will know what we're dealing with."

"Round up the boys, Sully. Let me make a call to the coroner, then Kirby and I will join you," Jim said. Jim had just finished making the call when two shots rang out.

"Where did that come from?" Jim asked.

"Somewhere on the other side of the mountain," Sully said. " I didn't know we had anyone over there this early."

"It may be the sheriff, boys," Jim said.

"They may have found the cave," Sully said.

"Have everyone saddle up, we'll get something to eat later," Jim said.

Jim's cell phone rang. "Hello," he said.

"This is Deputy Abel," the voice said, "we found something that could be the cave entrance on the side of a hill. We're considering blowing a hole in it."

"No, don't do that. It may cause a cave-in, and if they are in there, we will never get them out. Wait until we get there and we'll figure out a plan. Where are you?"

"On the west slope," he said. "You will run into us about halfway down on the slope."

"Okay, we're on our way," Jim said and hung up.

"Did they find the cave?" Kirby asked.

"Maybe. There's loose dirt on the side of a hill, on the west slope, that could be a covered up entrance. We'll go take a look. If it is, we'll call the mining company for some advice, they're used to dealing with things like that."

Sully and Jim saddled up and led their horses over to the hand's tent.

"Gather round," Sully said, "the sheriff's deputies may have found the cave."

Everyone cheered.

"Get saddled up as quickly as you can, we have to ride over to the west slope. I'll call Cookie and tell him to bring breakfast to us," Sully said.

Everyone scrambled for their saddles and horses.

"It would be a miracle if they're still alive," Kirby said.

"Everybody's entitled to one," Sully said.

24

After distancing themselves from the Rebs, Chris and Will continued to ride all night to reach Seven Stars by morning. At first light, they were almost there.

"We should be getting close," Will said.

"Good," Chris said, "I got a serious case of the hungry's, and we have to feed and water the horses."

They topped a hill and the sun was sitting on the roof of a tavern. "There it is," Will said, "that's the Blue Tail Tavern."

"Yeah, I see it," Chris said. "Why do they call it the Blue Tail Tavern?"

"I think it's for a bird in the region."

"What kind of bird?"

"I don't know, a blue tail bird. What difference does it make?"

"None, I just wondered."

A large two-story house, with a porch running all the way across the front, stood on a small hill with a sign next to the walkway that read 'Blue Tail Tavern.'

From the looks of the place, you would never know the destruction taking place twenty miles away. The paint on the tavern was a clean white, and flowers were growing along the walkway to the front door. Inside the windows were bright red drapes, bellowing down the sides of the windows. There was a big white barn nearby. It was like the place was surrounded by an invisible shield that protected it from the rest of the world.

"Why do they call this area Seven Stars?" Chris asked.

"Do I look like an encyclopedia?"

"Do you know?"

"Some say it's because that mountain range looks a lot like the one in China that's named Seven Stars. There are several stories, no one knows for sure. You happy now?"

"Yep."

As they rode closer to the tavern, a pretty young woman wearing a green shirt and jeans, with big blue eyes and red hair, appeared on the front porch carrying a 12 gauge shotgun with a strap on it, hung over her arm. She placed her hand to her brow to get a good look through the morning sun, as Chris and Will rode up to the hitching post.

She raised the shotgun and pointed it at Chris and Will.

"You Union or Confederate?" she asked.

"If I give the wrong answer, are you going to shoot me?" Chris asked.

"We have to protect our property."

"Is your family's last name Issery?" Will asked.

"Yes it is," she said.

"Then I think I can tell you we're Union," Will said. "We work for the Flying G, we're on our way home."

"I'm Jennie," she said and lowered the shotgun.

"Never seen anyone have a strap on a shotgun," Chris said.

"That's so no one can take it away from me. How did you know my name?"

"I read about your tavern and the others in Seven Stars, they're quite famous."

"Don't know anything about that," she said.

"Are you open for breakfast?" Will asked.

"Yes we are. It's twenty-five cents each for the meal, and another quarter a piece if you want to feed your horses. If you want to spend the night, that's fifty cents more each, provided my Pa agrees."

"Good," Will said, "you take a federal twenty-dollar gold piece?"

"Come on in," she said, and took the strap of the shotgun off her arm.

Will and Chris got down off their horses, tied them to the hitching post, and walked in. The inside looked as good as the outside. A long mahogany dining table with twelve chairs ran the length of the room. A harpsichord was in a corner, and a stone fireplace filled the rest of the wall, with a picture of President Lincoln hanging over the fireplace.

Several black leather chairs, end tables, and a long red couch that matched the drapes completed the room.

"Have a seat," she said. "I got eggs, pork belly, biscuits, coffee, or water. That be all right?"

"That sounds great, I'll have water," Chris said.

"Me too," Will said.

Jennie turned away and walked through a swinging door into a kitchen, carrying her shotgun. About thirty minutes later, she came back through the door carrying two plates and two glasses of water on a tray. She sat the tray on the table and handed Chris and Will their plates and water. "Your utensils are on the table," she said. "I'll go get my Papa, be right back."

A few minutes later a door opened, and Jennie pushed a wheelchair through the open door, with a haggard-looking man in it. He was wearing a Union Army officer's cap, with red hair spilling out the sides. His legs had been cut off above the knees and a Model One Smith and Wesson pistol was lying in his lap. His eyes looked tired and knowing, as only a man with his experiences could.

Jennie pushed the wheelchair up to the table. "Howdy, gents, my name's Thomas Issery," he said. "I own the place."

"I'm Will, and this is Chris," Will said.

"This is my Pa," Jennie said, "he's a hero."

His blue eyes brightened and the corners of his parched lips turned into a slow smile. "My daughter tends to exaggerate, I was doing my duty like everyone else. We fought Lee's Army to a standstill in Miller's cornfield at the Battle of Antietam in '62. Cost me my legs, and I was one of the lucky ones. You never forget the smell of death, the stench is still hanging in the air there like a dirty curtain. It was the bloodiest battle of the war so far."

"Sorry about your legs," Will said.

"That's the fortunes of war. I had a lot of plans for this place, but the war has changed everything."

"Your family has owned the tavern for a long time, haven't they?" Will asked.

"For fifty years. It's been around for a hundred, but you're our last guest. We let the staff go a week ago. The Battle at Gettysburg will spill over to here soon, and I don't want my daughter here when it does. I lost my wife to pneumonia last winter, Jennie lost her husband at Chancellorsville, and I'm good as dead. She's the only one left. She said you're from the Flying G. I know Mr. Goodman, he used to stay here before the war, when he was waiting for cattle from Kansas. He's a good honorable man. I would think if you work for him, you would be too."

"We hope we are," Chris said. "All the Goodmans are good people."

"Here's your money," Will said, handing Jennie the gold piece. "We want to water and feed our horses too, keep the change."

"Give him his money back, child, it's on the house," Issery said. "We want to pay," Chris said.

"Not this time. Jennie, would you mind fixing a pot of coffee?"

"Sure, Papa," she said, and handed Will back the money and hurried away. Issery watched her disappear into the kitchen. "I have a proposition for you," he said. "If you will take Jennie with you to the Flying G, I'll pay you whatever you want."

"We can't do that," Chris said.

"You don't understand, sir," Will said, "we're not from your time, we don't belong here. She can't go with us."

"I can't let the Rebs get her. You know what I'm saying, name your price."

"Why don't you just get a wagon and leave?"

"How long do you think I would last out there with no legs? I may be able to survive here, because even the enemy respects a fallen soldier, but Jennie won't because she's a woman. I sure can't protect her. You're her last hope."

Jennie came through the kitchen door again. "Here's your coffee, Papa." She sat a cup down on the table and poured the coffee.

"Thank you, child, I do appreciate it," he said. "Why don't you play the boys a song on the harpsichord? "

"I can't play in front of anybody, Pa," she said, blushing.

"We really don't have time anyway," Chris said. "We have an appointment we have to keep."

"I'll show you where the horse feed is," she said and started for the door.

"Looks like I was wrong about you two," Issery said.

"It's impossible," Will said. "I'm sorry."

"What's going on?" Jennie asked, looking surprised.

"Nothing," Issery said, "take them to the barn."

Will and Chris went back outside with Jennie, untied their horses, and led them to the barn.

"That's a good looking Appaloosa," Chris said as they walked in the barn.

"He belongs to my Pa. He's a war horse," she said.

"We have to make this quick," Chris said, "you-know-who should be here anytime."

"What was going on with Pa?" Jennie asked. "Ya'll got some kind of secret?"

"No," Will said, "he was worried about you staying here with all the fighting going on. I think you already knew that."

"We got no place else to go," she said.

"That seems to be a common problem with everyone these days," Will said.

"If you don't mind, we'll take a small sack of grain with us," Chris said.

"Take what you need. I got some biscuits left if you want to take them too." Chris glanced at Will and smiled, "No thank you, but we appreciate it."

They were feeding the horses when a group of Union soldiers rode by, not very far away, leading four pack mules going the wrong way. Gettysburg was behind them.

"That's got to be them," Chris said.

"Yeah, I never thought it would really happen," Will said.

"He doesn't have the gold yet, there's nothing on the mules," Chris said. "Who you talking about?" Jennie asked.

"Some bad people," Will said. "We got to go, Jennie, we'll walk you back in the house and say a quick goodbye to your Pa. You should leave too. Make him go with you to someplace that's safe. They will be back, and they are trouble."

Chris and Will left their horses eating and closed the barn door. When they went in the house, Thomas Issery had his wheelchair pulled up to the dining room table, with two small leather sacks sitting in front of him.

"There's ten thousand dollars in those sacks, gentlemen. It's yours if you will take Jennie with you," he said.

"I'm not going anywhere without you," Jennie said. "You have to, child, it's the only way. These two can get you to a safe place and a chance to start over. I think I can trust them to do that."

She ran to her pa, dropped to her knees, and hugged him. "I would rather die than leave you," she said. "I won't go."

"You have to," he said.

"Mr. Issery, there's no way we can explain it, but we can't take Jennie with us. It has nothing to do with money. If we had bad intentions, we would take it anyway. She can't go where we're going," Chris said.

The front door opened, and Kaman stood in the doorway. He walked in, and the soldier that followed him was bigger, dirtier, and ornery-looking, the kind that would pull the legs off grasshoppers to watch them spin.

"Unbelievable," Will said. "It's quite a shock to see him standing there after what has happened."

"Yeah, makes the hair stand up on your neck, doesn't it," Chris said. "He looks a little better than the last time we saw him, but not much, and that dude with him looks like he's already a zombie."

"You know these men?" Issery asked.

"Kind of," Chris said, "they're deserters."

"I don't know you," Kaman said. "Shut your mouth. We did our time, now it's someone else's turn. My boys will be here soon, and they're going to be powerfully hungry. Get in the kitchen, little lady, and cook up a mess of vittles in a hurry."

"We're closed," Issery said.

"Well, you're going to open back up," Kaman said.

The ornery cuss was eyeing Jennie, until he saw the two sacks on the table. "What you got in them sacks, mister?" he asked. "None of your business," Issery said.

"That wouldn't be gold, would it?" he said.

"Let's have a look," Kaman said.

"Get out of my house, you cowards," Issery said. "A dead man don't need gold," the ornery cuss said and went for his pistol. Chris drew and fired, putting a bullet right between his eyes before he touched his holster, then turned the Colt on Kaman.

"Don't kill him, Chris, we need him," Will said.

"That's a mighty quick draw you got," Kaman said. "You can ride along with us if you have a mind to. I never liked him anyway."

The sound of horses approaching got everyone's attention.

"Sounds like my boys are back, loaded and ready to go," Kaman said. "It's over. Now, put that pistol down, boy, you're outnumbered. You can back off, or we'll kill you and take that little girl with us."

Jennie picked up a table knife and charged Kaman. He knocked the knife out of her hand, grabbed her and pulled her in front of him, drew his pistol, and shot Issery through the heart. Jennie screamed and struggled to get free from Kaman.

"That should give you something else to think about," he said, pushed Jennie away, and darted out the door, yelling, "You're dead, all of you are dead!" Jennie ran to her Pa, fell to her knees, and hugged him. Blood was running into his lap, over the Model One, and dripping on the floor.

"I should have shot him," Chris said. "I could have got him."

"If you kill him, we will never get back," Will said and bolted the door.

"Right now, I don't care," Chris said.

"We may not get out of here anyway," Will said. "Take him down if you have to, I'm with you."

Jennie let out a furious scream, reached in her Papa's lap, picked up the bloody Model One, and ran for the door. "I'll kill him. I swear I'll kill him," she said.

Will ran and grabbed her before she could open the door. "What are you doing?" he asked. "You think your Pa would want you to get killed? Give me the gun."

"No," she said, "I've got to kill him."

"There's too many of them," Chris said. "You will be the one that gets killed, you understand? There's nothing you can do to help your Pa except stay alive. We'll get him, but not now."

Tears rolled down her cheeks. She took a deep breath, wiped her eyes, and handed Chris the gun. "You're right. I have to stay alive so I can kill that son of a bitch."

She walked to the table, picked up the two sacks of gold. "Come with me," she said, and hurried through the swinging kitchen door to the kitchen pantry and opened it. She picked up her shotgun, put the stock strap on her arm, picked up the saddle bags, and put the gold in them. She reached back in the saddle bags and took out two shotgun shells, cracked the shotgun breech, and loaded it. "There's a tunnel that leads from the kitchen to the barn," she said, "it's been there for a hundred years. I think we can still get through it." She pulled a lever behind the stove, and a door came open that was nailed to the pantry.

"Just like in the movies," Chris said, staring at the door.

"Maybe I am lucky," Will said. "You can come along for the ride."

"Wait," she said, and ran back into the dining room. She came back pushing Thomas Issery in the wheel chair, with a blanket over him. "Take him in there."

Chris pushed the wheelchair through the open doorway. A huge walk-in iron safe was standing inside the door. She reached down and spun the dial a couple of times, opening the safe.

"Put him in the safe, it will be his mausoleum."

Chris pushed the chair into the safe. She picked up two more sacks of gold and a small box, put it in the saddle bags, and closed the door and spun the dial.

"Rest in peace, Papa," she said and pulled the pantry door closed. They made their way through the tunnel to the barn, and quickly saddled their horses.

"I thought we weren't going to do this," Will said.

"Do we have a choice?" Chris asked.

"No," Will said.

They heard a crash, and knew Kaman and his gang had knocked the front door down.

"Okay, Jennie," Chris said. "When we open the barn door, you have to ride like never before. And remember, not now, this is not the time, stay with us. Here, you might need this." He took the Model One out of his belt and handed it to her.

"Thanks," she said. "I got something special to do with this."

"I think the appaloosa can stay close. Don't slow down until we do."

"Spot can outrun your horses," she said.

"His name is spot?" Chris asked.

"He's an appaloosa, what else?" she said.

"Get on your horse," Chris said. They mounted and took off like a streak of lightning, out of the barn and over the hill, while Kaman and his gang searched for them inside the house.

The appaloosa was running neck and neck with Spot number one and Rover as they disappeared into the trees, a hundred yards away.

25

Chris raised his hand for a signal to slow down and they slowed the horses to a walk. Jennie turned in the saddle and took one last look toward her home. They could see flames devouring what had been a hundred-year-old part of history. "I knew they would burn it. People like that don't want anyone to have something they don't."

"Sorry," Will said. "Nothing you can do now except go on. Your Pa wanted to save you from that, you just barely made it."

"I don't care anymore," she said. "I got one mission, and that's to kill that no-good that murdered my Pa."

"He's on our radar too," Will said.

"On your what?" she asked.

"What he means is, we have to plan how and when to do it," Chris said. "We know he will be going to the Flying G mountains."

"What did he do to you?" she asked.

"It's too complicated to explain," Will said. "You should have let me kill him, I don't care what happens to me," she said.

"Your daddy did, and you would be doing him a disservice if you didn't try to live," Chris said.

"I don't want to talk about it anymore right now," she said. "What do we do know?"

"Find a place with some water and rest for a while, and then move on toward the Flying G before Kaman gets there."

"His name is Kaman?" she asked.

"Yes," Chris said, "Ernest Kaman."

"I'll remember that."

They stopped beside a little creek, unsaddled and watered the horses, sat down under a tree, and ate some biscuits Jennie brought in her saddle bags with no complaints.

"We're very sorry about what's happened to your family," Will said.

"It's a terrible time," Chris said.

"Brad and I had been married six months," she said. She lifted up a locket from a chain around her neck, and opened it for Chris and Will to see. "This is Brad."

"Nice looking young man," Chris said.

"Sure is," Will said.

"He was a lieutenant in General Hooker's command," she said. "Lee's Army destroyed his unit at Chancellorsville. I got a telegram saying he was a brave soldier, and was killed on the battlefield and buried there. That was two months ago. I don't know who killed my husband, but I do know who killed my Pa, and I intend to kill him…with or without your help." She got up, wiped a tear away. "I'm going to cool off." She walked down to the creek. She took off her boots, shirt, and jeans, and got into the creek in her underwear.

Chris and Will tried to look away, but the sight of a beautiful young woman brought their eyes back to the creek.

"That's quite a young lady," Will said.

"Yeah, she sure is," Chris said. "Shame about her husband."

"It sure is," Will said. "Have you thought about what happened back there?"

"Some," Chris said.

"We almost killed Kaman," Will said. "Yet, we know that wouldn't have happened because we found him in a cave a hundred and fifty years later."

"Kind of boggles the mind, doesn't it," Chris said. "I'm still convinced we wouldn't be here if it hadn't been for Kaman. We have to follow him through whatever happens when he gets to the mountain for us to return to our time."

"What do we do with Jennie?" Will asked. "We can't take her with us."

"Or can we?" Chris said.

"I don't think so."

"Are you sure about that?" Chris asked.

"I don't know what's going to happen anymore than you do. I'm trying to apply a little logic."

"With what's happened to us, I don't think there is such a thing."

"She would have to know the truth," Will said. "How do we do that? She may not want to go."

"Now that we know Kaman actually stole the gold, we have to concentrate on getting to the mountain, and deal with Jennie when the time comes. We'll play it by ear as they say," Chris said.

"Oh that's definitely a plan," Will said.

Jennie got out of the creek and put her clothes on, tied her long red hair into a ponytail, and walked back to Chris and Will.

"Feel better?" Will asked.

"Yes. Shouldn't we be moving on?"

"Yes we should," Chris said. "We got a jump on Kaman, we better keep it that way. Saddle up."

"How do you know he won't go somewhere else?" she asked.

"He won't, trust me," Will said. "We just have to get there by the time he does." She stuck the Model One in her jeans and hung the shotgun strap over the saddle horn, it dropped down on the side of the saddle, and she climbed on. "Let's go get Kaman," she said.

26

They rode along inside the tree line in silence, listening to the Battle of Gettysburg twenty miles away. Artillery fire echoed across the miles, and black smoke drifted overhead and disappeared in the hot July sky.

"Sounds like the battle is in full swing," Will said, "but it will get worse. Tomorrow there will be cannons lined up for two miles on both sides, and the fire will last for hours and hours. It will be the biggest artillery barrage in the history of war."

"How do you know that?" Jennie asked.

"I just do," Will said.

"He does a lot of reading," Chris said. "I'm not sure he gets it all right."

"You wouldn't know," Will said.

"I'm getting hungry. You got any more of those biscuits, Jennie?"

"No, we ate them all," she said.

"Mr. History, do you know if there's any place to get something to eat along the way?" Chris asked.

"I don't have a clue," Will said, "we should be close to Morganville in another couple of hours."

"I may can last that long," Chris said.

"You still got the letter Bain gave you?" Will asked.

"I got it."

"Good, you can give his wife the letter and stuff your face."

"You two sure talk in riddles sometimes," Jennie said.

"He does," Will said, "I think I'm pretty clear."

"As clear as a stained glass window," Chris said.

"I don't understand how you're so sure he will go to that mountain," she said.

"He will, I guarantee it," Will said. "Maybe we will try to explain why we are so sure later."

"Maybe," Chris said.

The sun was sitting on two o'clock in the afternoon when they saw Morganville in the distance.

"We better move in slow, in case Kaman is there," Chris said. "Jennie, you tag along behind so we can cover you."

"I don't think so. Me and this shotgun have our own plans," she said.

"You can't ride in shooting, even if Kaman is there." Will said. "We don't want to kill any of the wrong people."

"If Kaman is there, I'm going to kill him," she said.

"You can't do that," Will said, "we need him alive for a little longer."

"Why? I thought you wanted him dead too?"

"We'll let you know when," Chris said. "It better be soon," she said.

As they rode into town, they saw red, white, and blue Fourth of July banners hanging from the stores, and nobody on the street. They rode past the closed doors of the livery stable to the saloon. "Maybe Kaman has already been here," Will said.

"I hope not," Chris said.

The swinging doors of the saloon opened and the marshal stepped out on the sidewalk. "What are you two doing back here?" he asked, as they rode up to the hitching post.

"We're on our way back to the Flying G. This is our friend Jennie, she's the daughter of Thomas Issery, he owned the Blue Tail Tavern in Seven Stars. A bunch of deserters burned it down and murdered him."

"Name's Longley, Miss Issery. I'm the marshal here. I'm sorry to hear about your Pa. I've visited your place."

"I'm a widow, Mr. Longley, my married name is Harris. My husband was Army Lieutenant Bradley Harris, he was killed at Chancellorsville."

"The war has left a lot of widows. I'm sorry for your loss, ma'am," Longley said.

"Where is everybody?" Will asked.

"Most are in the saloon. We're having a town meeting, getting ready for Independence Day."

"Just a bit premature, aren't you?" Will said.

"The war is about over," Longley said. "General Meade will chase them Johnny Rebs clear back to Alabama."

Chris looked at Will and shook his head no.

"I wasn't going to say anything," Will said.

"Where can we get something to eat?" Chris asked.

"You might try the saloon, the hotel diner is closed until the meeting is over. Brute's in the saloon, he can put your horses up for you if you're going to stay."

"We're going to stay," Jennie said. "Long enough to eat," Chris said.

They got down off their horses, tied them, and went in the saloon. The saloon looked the same as it did before, except there were more people. The bartender had a shiner on his right eye, and Miss Kitty was wearing pants and boots. "Well if it isn't the boys from yesterday," Miss Kitty said. "You ever figure out what year it was?"

"Unfortunately, yes," Will said.

"Can you fix us something to eat, Miss Kitty, I'm starving," Chris said.

"I can do that. Who's this pretty little thing?" she asked, looking at Jennie.

"Jennie Harris," Chris said, "this is Miss Kitty. Jennie, she owns the place."

Jennie smiled and nodded hello.

"Would you be looking for a job?" Kitty asked. "With your looks, you could do well here."

"No ma'am, thank you," Jennie said.

"That's too bad," Kitty said. "I'll have Bobbie fix you all a steak, cost you five bucks a piece."

"Sounds good to me," Chris said.

"Be about thirty minutes," she said. "Have a drink, it's on the house."

They sat down and the bartender brought Chris and Will water.

"What happened to that eye?" Will asked.

"Had a drunk that didn't take too kindly to being thrown out. What will you have, young lady?" he asked.

"I'll have some red wine if you have it."

"Sure do, I save it for the ladies. I'll be right back." The bartender brought a bottle of red wine and a crystal wine glass, sat them on the table, and poured the wine.

"Thank you," Jennie said and raised the glass toward the bartender. He smiled.

"Do you know where I can find Barbara Bain?" Chris asked.

"She works here," he said, "everyone calls her Bobbie."

"Really?" Chris asked.

"Yeah, she's fixing your steaks. She's the cook." he said.

"That's a relief," Will said.

"What do you mean?" he asked.

"Nothing," Will said.

"I have something for her," Chris said. "I'll go get it, it's in my saddle bags."

"Okay, I'll tell her," he said and walked away.

Chris hurried away, and was back in a flash with the letter.

A petite little girl, with big blue eyes and long brown hair, came out of the kitchen carrying a tray with three plates of sizzling steaks. She had a white apron on over the bright blue dress that matched her eyes.

"I think this is for you," she said, and sat the plates on the table. "I'm Bobbie. Fats said one of you had something for me?"

"I do," Chris said. "I have a letter from your husband. He asked me to deliver it. He's fine."

"Oh my goodness, you have a letter from Terry?"

"Yes ma'am I do," he said and handed her the letter.

She took the letter and held it to her breast, and tears ran down her cheeks. "Excuse me," she said, and ran to the kitchen door and went in.

"I'm glad I got to do that," Chris said.

"That was nice of you," Jennie said.

"Yep. You did good, partner," Will said.

In a few minutes she was back, holding the opened letter in her hand. "Which one of you is Christopher Bain?" she asked.

"I am," Chris said.

"My husband said you saved his life and he owes you a debt of gratitude. I'm pregnant; he knows, and said he wants to name our baby Christopher if it's a boy, if that's alright with you."

"I'm speechless," Chris said.

"Just say yes," Will said.

"Yeah, that's quite an honor," Jennie said.

"Sure, it's okay with me," Chris said.

"Good," Bobbie said, "is this your wife?"

"She's a friend," Chris said.

"What's your name, Miss?" she asked.

"Jennifer. They call me Jennie," she said.

"Okay, if it's a boy, his name is Christopher," Bobbie said. "If it's a girl, her name is Jennifer. That okay with everyone?"

"Now I'm speechless," Jennie said. "Thank you."

"I'll write Terry tonight and tell him, he will be very happy. Are you going to be staying for a while?"

"No, we have to be moving on after we eat," Chris said.

"Thank you for bringing me the letter," she said. "You have made me very happy."

"You're welcome," Chris said. "Thank you."

"Goodbye," she said and walked away.

They finished off the steaks and walked outside, untied their horses, mounted, and rode down the street.

"What you thinking, Hopalong?" Will asked. "Do we wait for Kaman?"

"Why did you call him that?" Jennie asked.

"It's a joke, I was kidding," Will said.

"I have been thinking about that," Chris said.

"About the joke?" Jennie asked.

"No, about whether we should wait for Kaman, or go on to the mountain. I don't think he's ahead of us, and he would probably stop here for supplies, but maybe not. I think we should go on to the mountain and be waiting when he gets there."

"I agree," Will said. "What do we do about Jennie?"

"That's a problem I haven't figured out yet," Chris said. "Don't worry about me. I'm going to kill Kaman and then try to find Brad's grave and have him moved to our family graveyard…and bury my Pa."

"I don't think you will have much luck with that," Will said. "Most of the graves on the battlefield are mass graves. There are so many, they dig a big hole and put a lot of bodies in one grave with no markers."

"Why don't you let us take care of Kaman for you, and you go on home," Chris said.

"No, not until Kaman is dead," she said.

"We need him alive until we get to the mountain," Will said.

"There you go, talking in riddles again," she said. "What difference does it make where we kill him, as long as we do."

"It's hard to explain, even I don't believe it sometimes," Will said.

"Try me," she said.

"What do you think, Chris?" Will asked.

"Let's think about it some more."

"What's the big secret?" she asked.

"We'll let you know when the time is right," Chris said. A lone rider appeared, riding hard in to town. He rode up to the saloon, jumped off his horse, started yelling for the marshal, and ran in the saloon.

"Wonder what that's all about," Will said.

"He was riding like the Devil was chasing him," Jennie said.

They turned their horses back to the saloon, dismounted, and went in. The rider was talking to the marshal.

"There's a bunch of renegades coming," he said. "There's Rebel and Union soldiers riding together. They ain't coming for the celebration."

"They will try to pick this town apart," Longley said. "Charlie, stop playing that infernal piano," he yelled, "I'm trying to talk!" The piano player stopped playing and turned on the piano stool to face the marshal.

"Listen up," Longley said, "everyone, get your guns and take cover. If they come into this town, they will wish they hadn't."

"Sounds like Kaman is on his way," Will said.

"I don't think so. He wouldn't want to share the gold with anyone else, and there wasn't any rebels riding with him at Seven Stars, and there are more of them."

"If it is Kaman, what do we do if someone kills him?" Will asked.

"Someone is going to kill him," Jennie said. "Me."

"We'll wait and see and play it---" Will interrupted Chris, "I know, play it by ear, right?" he said.

"I got to find another expression," Chris said.

"Let's put the horses in the livery stable, get our rifles, and find cover," Will said.

"This shotgun can hardly wait," Jennie said.

"I think it was your idea to bring her along," Chris said. "I didn't hear any objections out of you," Will said.

"I hear hoof beats," Jennie said, "we better hurry."

They rode to the livery stable, opened the door, led the horses in, got their weapons, and closed the door.

"This may be the beginning of the end for us," Will said. "We could be stuck here for the rest of our lives if we survive this."

"Jennie, you still got time to ride out of here," Chris said.

"No way, I'm staying," she said.

"We should have never gone to that mountain," Will said.

"I told you not to come," Chris said.

"I know, bad decision," Will said.

27

A big yellow truck with a long trailer and a drilling rig on it pulled up beside Jim's truck and stopped. It had a sign on the door that read 'Weatherford Mining Company.' A man wearing a safety hat, yellow company shirt, jeans, and work boots got out of the truck and walked over to where Jim and Sully were standing.

"Ken Stratton," he said and reached out a hand to shake with them, "the boss said there was two men trapped in a cave."

"We think so. We think that's a cave behind you, and the entrance has caved in," Jim said. "We didn't want to do anything that would endanger them. That's why I called you."

"How long they been in there?" Ken asked.

"We don't know for sure, maybe four days or more," Jim said.

"I hate to tell you this, but if they have been in there that long, they may be dead already."

"I want to get them out either way," Jim said.

"Okay, I did some checking, and I think what you're referring to is an old copper mine that was abandoned in 1850."

"I told you I had seen it, boss," Sully said.

"What do we do now?" Jim asked.

"The first thing is to drill an air hole from the top, and then figure out how to get them out. It might be safer to drill a hole from the top, big enough to send someone down to check, but that will take some time. I don't think it would be safe to go into the caved-in entrance. They didn't reinforce these old mines, and the whole thing could fall in."

"You're the expert," Jim said.

"The rest of my crew will be here soon. I'll have them drill an air hole down as fast as they can, and go from there. I need everyone to stay out of the way."

"How long will it take?" Sully asked.

"It's going to be dark soon. We'll have to set up lights first, then about two hours after that to drill the air hole. To get a hole big enough to get them out, another twenty-four to thirty hours."

"That's a long time," Jim said, "can't you do anything to speed it up?"

"I'm sorry, no. If we go too fast it could be disastrous."

"I want them out," Jim said.

"We'll get them out, but I can't guarantee they will be alive."

"I know. Do the best you can," Jim said.

Ken walked back to his truck and slipped on a pair of rubber boots. Out of the corner of his eye, he saw what he thought was a ragged-looking man standing at the back of his truck. When he turned to get a better look, he was gone. He walked to the back of the truck, and there was no one there.

Two Suburbans pulled up beside his truck and six men got out of each one, with miner's hats on. A big man in his forties with a beer belly walked over to Ken. "What's the story, boss?"

"We got to drill an air hole into the top of that hill, then dig a bigger hole and rig up an elevator," he said, pointing at the hill. "There may be two men trapped inside, according to Jim Goodman. Make sure you keep everyone away except our crew. I think I saw someone snooping around my truck already."

28

The setting sun crawled across the horizon, silhouetting the riders as they rode into town. A Rebel captain was at the front, with about twenty Rebel soldiers and eight to ten Union soldiers mixed in. Kaman was nowhere to be seen, this was a different bunch.

Seeing the streets were empty, the captain halted the soldiers and divided them into two groups. One group stayed put, and the other one circled the town and lined up at the other end of the only town street.

When the soldiers were in place, the captain moved his horse forward from the group and stopped. "I'm Captain Theodore Brown, you have five minutes to show yourself. We need supplies, food, and water. You can cooperate and we will ride out with no one hurt. If you don't, we will kill anyone that gets in our way and burn the town. The clock's ticking."

A voice from inside the saloon yelled out, "You ain't soldiers, you deserters!"

"We're a Confederate detail on a mission to take these Yankee prisoners to a prison camp. We have no desire to kill civilians, unless it is absolutely necessary to the success of our mission. Don't make us do it," he said.

Chris, Will, and Jennie were looking through the crack in the livery stable door, at the Confederate captain. It was hard to make out his face in the dwindling light of day. "We can't let them take those prisoners to a prison camp," Jennie said.

"This is not our town, we can't make the decision on what to do here," Will said.

"I can't see them very good," Chris said, "but it looks like all the Union soldiers are officers. I see two colonels, and it looks like some lower ranking men too. Their hands are tied to the saddle horn and their feet to the stirrups, with a lead rope to a soldier."

"We got to rescue them," Jennie said.

"Will, you been talking about how fast we can fire these rifles, maybe it's time to put them to the test," Chris said

"You're not really suggesting we walk out there like Gunsmoke and get our ass shot off?"

"Only if the townspeople don't do anything," Chris said. "Jennie's right, we can't let them take the prisoners. We don't belong here, but this may be the one thing we do that makes any sense for us being here."

"You're kind of like Custer," Will said, "more guts than brains. I should have taken that airport job for the summer."

"Look at this," Jennie said, peeking through the cracks.

Will and Chris placed their eyes to the opening and saw the marshal standing on the sidewalk in front of the saloon, holding a white flag.

"Looks like he's surrendering the town," Jennie said. "What are we going to do?"

"Can you hear me, Captain?" the marshal asked.

"I hear you," he said.

"There's no sense in getting a bunch of people killed. If you will release the prisoners, we will give you what you need, and you can go on your way."

"No deal," the captain said. "We don't need them if we can't complete our mission. Your time's up, we're coming in. Get out of our way."

Chris stepped out of the livery stable door with an empty holster and no rifle. "Captain, over here," he said.

The captain turned his head toward the livery stable.

"What you got to say?" the captain asked. "You better make it quick."

"I got expert riflemen with repeater rifles pointed at you. Watch the diner sign," Chris said.

Four bullets hit the sign in less than five seconds.

"That don't prove anything," the captain said. "You're outgunned, Captain. Give us the prisoners and ride away," Chris said.

"Don't forget we're here too, Captain," the marshal said. "Everybody, outside," the marshal said, and people started coming out from everywhere with their rifles at the ready.

A sergeant behind the captain moved his horse forward beside him. "I've seen those repeaters in action, Captain, that wasn't no Springfield. We'll get off a few rounds before they kill us all, but we're no match for them," he said.

The captain shook his head and looked at Chris. "If you shoot, we will kill the prisoners. Put a gun to their head, boys."

The soldiers placed their rifle barrels to the prisoners' heads and cocked the hammers.

"It looks like we have a Mexican standoff," he said. "It's getting dark and I have run out of patience. What's it going to be?"

The sound of horses running brought everyone to silence as they listened to the oncoming sound.

A Rebel soldier rode up to the captain. "There's a bunch of Yankee soldiers coming, Captain. There's too many now, we got to get out of here."

"What's your orders, Captain?" the sergeant asked.

The captain didn't say anything for several seconds, then looked at the sergeant. "Turn the prisoners loose and ride," he said.

The sergeant turned his horse, facing the soldiers. "Drop the lead ropes on the prisoners and ride out," he said.

They let go of the ropes and spurred their horses into a run. The captain turned his horse to face Chris. "Next time will be our time," he said and rode away.

"We did it," Jennie said, "we rescued the prisoners."

"Maybe," Chris said. "I don't think that's soldiers coming, it's got to be Kaman's bunch. We're not out of the woods yet."

"I'll go tell the marshal who they are," Will said.

"Jennie and I will help with the prisoners," Chris said. "We have to get them out of sight."

Chris helped a tired, skinny colonel off his horse and handed him a canteen of water. "I never thought I would see a friendly face again," the colonel said. "My name's Woods. Thank you."

"We still have a problem, Colonel," Chris said. "A bunch of deserters I have dealt with before are coming. We have to get ready for them."

Several of the townspeople escorted prisoners to the saloon. Brute carried one to the saloon that was too weak to walk.

Jennie was untying one of the soldier's hands when she looked up at him, stepped back, stared at him for a moment in the dim light, and fainted.

The soldier slid off his horse, went to her, and held her in his arms.

"Oh my god, it is you," he said. "I thought I would never see you again, Jennie. Wake up, sweetheart."

Chris came over and dropped to his knees beside them. "You're Brad?" he asked.

"Yes, this is my wife Jennie."

"I know, she thought you were dead."

"Who are you?" Brad asked.

"A friend," Chris said.

"What kind of friend?" Brad asked, looking suspicious.

"Not that kind," Chris said.

Jennie moaned and her eyes came open. She rubbed them and moved her head closer to him, and placed her hand on his face. "You're a dead ringer for my husband," she said.

Chris smiled, got up, and looked at Jennie. "It is him."

"Is it really you, Brad?" she asked. She sat up and put her arms around him. "I got a telegram saying you were dead, and they buried you on the battlefield."

"I was taken prisoner and led around like a monkey for the past two months with those other officers, to celebrate their victory at Chancellorsville," he said. "I got hit by canon shrapnel that knocked me out. I woke up with blood all over me, lying among the dead. Our soldiers must have thought I was dead. The Johnny Rebs came along, saw I was alive, and took me prisoner."

Will came running up. "The town's ready for them." He looked down and saw Jennie with her arms around the soldier.

"It's Brad," Chris said. "He's been a prisoner of war for the last two months."

"Well I'll be, it's a miracle," Will said.

"This is Chris and Will, Brad," Jennie said. "They helped me get away. Those men coming murdered my Pa and burned my house down. I have been waiting for them, it's payback time."

"Colonel, you and Brad come with us," Chris said. "We need to get back to the livery stable where the horses are. You coming Brute? It's your place."

"Right behind you," Brute said, and everyone hurried to the livery stable and closed the doors.

"Kaman's going to get blown away for sure now, maybe us with him," Will said.

"A good possibility," Chris said.

"I can't let anyone else kill him, I got to do it," Jennie said, and picked up her shotgun and checked the Model One.

"Brad, talk some sense into her," Will said, "she's determined to get killed."

"He's right, son," the colonel said. "You should take your wife out of here before the shooting starts. After all you both been through, you don't want to die like this."

"You can get out the back of the livery stable and be gone before they know it, if you will go now," Chris said. "We'll take care of Kaman, I promise."

"Anyone got a pencil and paper?" Colonel Woods asked.

"I got a pen," Will said. He took a ballpoint pen from his pocket.

"Here's some paper," Brute said and handed him a sheet of paper.

"I never seen nothing like this," the colonel said, looking at the ballpoint pen.

"It's like a pencil," Will said, "what do you want it for?"

"I have the authority to grant the lieutenant a discharge as a result of his POW status, if he wants it. He's been a brave soldier, he has nothing else to prove."

Brad looked at Jennie, and took her hand. "They're right, Jennie. I don't want to lose you again."

Jennie held a look at Brad for a few seconds, then turned to Chris and Will. "You promise you will take care of Kaman for me?" she asked.

"If we stay alive long enough," Chris said.

"That's good enough for me," she said. "Let's go home Brad, I need to bury my Pa."

"Okay," Colonel Woods said, "I'll write it out and sign it. You fill in your serial number and complete name. Good luck."

"I'll help you saddle your horses," Chris said and picked up Jennie's saddle. He placed the blanket and saddle on the appaloosa, reached under its belly, pulled the girt up through the hoop and looped it tight, and Jennie hung her shotgun on the saddle.

By the time he had Jennie's horse saddled and bridled, Brad had his horse ready.

"Here," Jennie handed Will the Model One, "I have been saving this just for Kaman. See that he gets it three or four time in the belly," she said and smiled.

Will took the pistol and she hugged his neck. "Bye Jennie," he said.

"Goodbye, Will, I'll miss you and your crazy stories."

"I'll miss you too," he said.

She put her arms around Chris and hugged him. "We did good, Chris," she said.

"Yes we did, take care," Chris said. "You better go now."

Brad shook the man's hand. "I can't thank you enough," he said. "If you're around here after the war, look us up."

"We may be," Will said.

Brad and Jennie climbed up in the saddle. Jennie looked down at Chris. "By the way," she said, "I was holding Spot back when we made our run, I didn't want to embarrass you," she said.

Chris smiled, opened the livery stable backdoor, and they rode into the night.

Someone rattled the front livery stable door. "Anyone in there?" a voice asked. "Unlock the door."

Chris peeked through the cracks. "There's only one out there," he whispered, "I'm going to open the door. When he comes in, you use that rifle stock on him, Will."

Will nodded.

Chris unlocked the door and opened it part way, he stood in the doorway where the soldier could see him. "What do you want?" Chris asked.

He drew his pistol and pointed it at Chris. "Drop that pistol on the ground real slow," he said.

Chris dropped the Colt on the ground and stepped back from the door, he rode through the half-opened door. Will stepped out from behind, and slammed the rifle stock against his head. He wobbled in the saddle a bit then fell off his horse, out cold.

Brute drug him to a stall, while Will and Chris tied his hands and feet and stuck the colonel's dirty bandana in his mouth

"This one was probably sent ahead to check things out," Will said. "I hope Kaman doesn't come in shooting when he doesn't come back."

"Colonel, you got a horse and weapons now, why don't you leave too," Chris said.

"I don't have a wife. You need all the firepower you can get," he said.

"This is a same song, second verse thing," Will said. "We get rid of one bunch and we got another."

"Yes it is," Chris said, "and it could work again."

"Jennie was right," Will said. "We do talk in riddles, especially you."

"I was thinking about a way to get Kaman out of here," Chris said.

"Did you say Kaman?" Colonel Woods asked.

"Yes, he's a deserter and stole a shipment of gold from the Union."

"I know him," the colonel said. "He was a company platoon sergeant in one of my companies before he disappeared."

"Would he know you?" Chris asked.

"I'm sure he would," the colonel said.

"Does he know you were captured?" Chris asked.

"I don't think so."

"What are you getting at?" Will asked.

"Kaman said there were soldiers after him on his way to the mountain. If that's true, we may can expedite his departure from Morganville if he thinks they're here. The colonel said Kaman would know him. What other reason would the colonel have for being here other than chasing Kaman? He doesn't know he was taken prisoner. It's dark, he can't tell how many men are here. We make a little noise to help the colonel out, the colonel gives him an ultimatum to surrender, he hightails it out of here, and we follow him to the mountain."

"It's worth a try," the colonel said. "If we wait for daylight, we don't have any choice but to fight."

"As crazy as it sounds, it might work," Will said. "But what if he wants to fight instead of run?"

"Then we fight," Chris said. "Colonel, you think you can sit a horse long enough to do this?"

"Put me on a horse," he said, "we may be able to save a lot of bloodshed. Someone else can worry about the gold."

"Kaman and his bunch will be here any time now," Chris said, "we'll let them come in. Colonel, you ride out where he can see you and call him out. Tell him you have him surrounded, and to surrender the gold. If they start shooting, get back to the livery stable as fast as you can."

"I'm ready," the colonel said. "Brute, go tell everyone to stay off the street, there's some bad guys coming, then back here," Chris said.

"You bet," Brute said and hurried away.

Chris and Will got the colonel on a horse, gave him a pistol, and waited for Kaman to arrive.

A little later, Brute came running into the livery stable. "They're here," he said.

A short time later they heard horses snorting, men talking. "I hope this works before somebody gets killed," Chris said.

"Mainly us," Will said.

They opened the livery stable doors and the colonel rode out.

"What if Kaman shoots him out of the saddle before he can run the bluff?" Will asked.

"Then we made a mistake," Chris said.

"No shit," Will said.

Colonel Woods stopped his horse and looked at the shadowy figures on the other side of the street, and yelled at Kaman. "Kaman, that you?" he asked.

A rider whirled his horse around to face the voice. "Yeah, who are you?"

"It's Colonel Woods, your commander. I have been waiting on you. They sent me to bring you and the gold back, you're surrounded."

"That figures, I knew somebody was after us. It doesn't surprise me it's you, I recognize your voice. I'll give you and your men a fifty-pound bar of gold if you will forget you saw us. You'll all be rich."

Out of the darkness, Will, Chris, and Brute started yelling. "Take the gold, Colonel, take the gold."

Several voices inside the saloon joined in and yelled, "We want some of it!"

"That's a lot of money," Kaman said. "Sounds like your men think so too."

"I agree," the colonel said, "I'm tired of working for nothing. Put the gold in front of the saloon and leave now. We'll tell them we couldn't find you."

"Deal," Kaman said. "But if you fire one shot, then the deal's off, and we start killing the locals: men, women, and children."

"Understood. Leave the gold and go, before I change my mind."

"Leroy, drop a bar of gold at the saloon and everyone ride out," Kaman said.

Leroy led a pack mule up to the saloon, pulled a strap, and a big burlap bag fell off the mule and made a thud sound as it hit the ground.

"There it is," Kaman said. "Now back off, we're riding out of here."

"Ride," the colonel said, and Kaman and the rest scattered, riding hard away from Morganville.

"That was an Academy Award performance, Colonel," Will said, as he and Chris walked out in the street.

"A what?" the colonel asked.

"I forgot, you wouldn't know about that," Will said. "You were great."

"Colonel, don't worry about Kaman. I can tell you for sure they will catch up to him. Goodbye, sir, and thanks. Brute, tell everyone goodbye for us, we have to keep up with Kaman. And tell Bobbie to take care of little Christopher."

"That's you?" Brute asked.

"Not exactly, she'll know what I mean."

The marshal walked out of the saloon and opened the burlap bag. "There's a big rock in the bag, he cheated us," he said. "Doesn't surprise me none," Chris said. "He thinks he got away with something."

"He probably had that planed for when he needed it," Will said. "He assumed the Army would know he stole the gold and would send someone after him."

"I would have had to turn it in," the colonel said. "I still have my honor."

"Thanks again, Colonel," Chris said. "We have to go now."

As Chris and Will entered the livery stable, a little black and tan hound puppy ran out of a stall, shaking his head, with a can stuck on his nose. Chris reached down, picked him up, and took the can off his nose. The puppy licked his hand to say thanks. "This your puppy, Brute?"

"No," Brute said. "He showed up here the other day, I don't know where he came from. You can have him if you want."

Chris looked at the sad-eyed little dog with long floppy ears. "You're going to get hurt if you stay around here," he said, and put the puppy in his saddle bags and climbed on his horse.

"You're going to take him with you?" Will asked.

"He needs a friend," Chris said, and they rode out of the livery stable.

Marshal Longley and Miss Kitty were standing in front of the saloon, watching them ride out. They waved goodbye and set out to catch up to Kaman, with a rising full moon leading the way.

29

Chris and Will rode along with their horses at a walk, letting them find their step in the darkness.

"I've been thinking," Will said.

"That's a first," Chris said.

"Somebody has to. How are we going to know what to do to get back when we get there? If we have to be in the cave, it may have caved in and we're shit out of luck. We don't know what Kaman's going to do. All we know for sure is he will go to the mountain, and he's still there as a zombie. Which reminds me of something else, I didn't think zombies talked, I thought all they did was look scary and eat people."

"There must be different kinds," Chris said, "Kaman talks a blue streak. Right now though, he's a live murderer, and we can't take any chances with him, before or after we get to the cave."

The puppy poked his head out of Chris's saddle bag and started whining.

"I think he needs to pee," Will said.

"Me too," Chris said, "let's make a pit stop." They reined their horses in and got off. Chris sat the puppy on the ground. He sniffed at the ground several times, squatted and peed, then looked up at Chris, who was relieving himself.

"I think he's hungry," Will said.

"Are you a dog whisperer now?"

"I was stating the obvious."

"Open one of those cans of ham," Chris said.

Will took his knife, cut the top of the can out, and handed it to Chris. Chris dipped his finger in the can, and came out with a big glob of ham on his finger and stuck it to the puppy's nose. The pup quickly licked the ham off Chris's finger and waited for more. Chris continued to feed him until his stomach was poked out like a basketball.

"What are you going to name him?" Will asked.

"Custer," Chris said.

"I like it. I think Custer would have too."

"If something happens to me, take him with you," he said, and put the pup back in his saddle bag.

"You don't have to ask. You know I would."

"It may be better to hold up here until it gets light," Chris said, "we don't know where Kaman is. We don't want to walk into an ambush."

"At first light, there's going to be a cannon barrage that will stretch for two miles from both sides," Will said. "It will last for almost a whole day. There will never be another one like it in the history of warfare."

"I've gained a whole new appreciation for the courage of the Civil War soldier, on both sides," Chris said. "Me too," Will said. "I realize now how good we have it. The ironic part about the cannon barrage is it happened on land owned by a free slave."

Spot started pawing the ground, switching his tail, and turning round and round as Chris hung on to the reins. "What's the matter with that crazy horse?" Will asked.

"I don't know. The only time I've seen him act like this was when there was a mare in season nearby."

"Way out here?" Will said. "I'm glad Rover's a gelding. I don't think he's glad, but I am."

"It could be a mare loose from one of the battles," Chris said.

"That's all we need," Will said. Chris reached in his saddle bags and lifted the puppy out. "Here, Will, put him in your bag until I get this horse settled down."

"Sure," Will said and took the pup from Chris, "you think he can come with us? He's not from the future."

"Now, why did you have to bring that up?"

"What, you never thought of it?"

"Give him back, he stays with me. If I go, he goes."

Will handed the pup back to Chris. "He just dribbled on me," Will said.

"That's not going to kill you," Chris said, and put the pup back in his saddle bags. He tightened one of the straps, and the pup squeezed his head out one side and barked. "Hush, Custer," Chris said.

Out of the darkness they heard a woman's voice. "What was that?" she asked. "That sounded like Miss Kitty," Will said.

Two riders came into view in the moonlight. It was the marshal and Miss Kitty.

"Don't shoot, it's Chris and Will," Will said. "What are you doing here?"

"We came for some of that gold," the marshal said, as they rode up beside Chris and Will.

Chris had to get a good grip on Spot's reins to keep him away from the mare, and the pup barked at them. Marshal Longley was riding a big bay gelding, dressed in black, with his single-action Colt strapped to his leg. Miss Kitty had a pearl-handled Remington pistol stuck in her black leather pants, sitting on a little mare about thirteen hands high with a blaze face named Betsy, who was causing all the trouble.

Spot tried to rear up, and Chris pulled him down and pushed the pup's head into the saddle bag.

"Can't you control that horse?" Miss Kitty asked.

"I don't see you doing a very good job either," Chris said.

"Marshal, you know better than to bring her out here," Will said. "Nothing but bad things are going to happen to both of you if you don't go home."

"I go where I want to go," she said. "Keep that animal away from my Betsy."

"I'm not going home without some of that gold," Longley said.

"You go up against Kaman, you won't be going home at all," Will said.

"We'll see," he said. "I didn't get to be a marshal by being timid."

"You've been warned," Chris said. "Do as you may, Mister Marshal."

Miss Kitty turned the mare around. "You coming or not, Longley?" she asked.

"I'm coming," he said, and spurred his horse to catch up to her.

Spot tried to pull away from Chris. He wrapped the reins around his hand several time and hung on. "Whoa, Spot, settle down. Not today," he said.

"Maybe we should wait until they get further away before we go," Will said.

"I think so. Maybe Spot will calm down. I think Custer's getting sea sick with all the bouncing."

"He'll be alright," Will said. "I'll help you keep an eye on him. It's not a good day for horse romance."

30

The first signs of morning light touched the faces of the exhausted drilling crew as it spread across the hilltop. Ken Stratton walked over to the elevator, and he and another man placed a big heavy bag on it. "Fire the engine up," he said, and the rig's engine came to life. He pushed a button on a cable and the elevator descended into the cave.

Jim and Sully walked up beside Ken. "It's been a long night," Jim said.

"It wasn't that deep, but we had to go through limestone to get there, so we had to go slow to keep it from caving it in. We busted through and hit the upper pocket early this morning. I'm checking the elevator out now. It won't be long before we can send someone down."

Kirby walked up and looked at the elevator. "I'll go down and get them," Jim said.

"Me too," Kirby said.

"I can't let you go. It has to be an employee, insurance requirements. If the elevator comes up alright, I'll send someone down to have a look. We piped the oxygen in yesterday, but it may have been too late. Our rescue may turn into a body recovery."

"Let's get on with it," Jim said. "I want them out of there either way." Ken punched the button again and the elevator rose to the top. Ken and the other man lifted the bag off the elevator and sat it on the platform. "I need a volunteer," Ken said.

Everyone looked at everyone else. A little man, with a pointed chin and big brown eyes, took off his steel hat and ran his fingers through his thinning hair. "I'll go boss," he said. "I don't weigh much, that should make it easier on the elevator."

"Yes it will. Thank you, Willie. Get your light and phone and we'll let you down. There's an oxygen bottle and a shovel on the elevator if you need them. If your phone doesn't work down there, tug on the rope three times when you get ready to come back up."

Willie got his miner's light and strapped it on his steel hat. He put the hat on his head, turned the light on, and stuck his cell phone in his pocket. "I'm ready," he said. "If something was to go wrong, tell my wife I love her."

"You'll be alright, we'll take good care of you," Ken said. Willie nodded and stepped on the elevator. "I hope they're alive," he said.

"We all do," Ken said and punched the button on the cable. Seconds later, the elevator dropped out of sight on its journey to the bottom of the mine shaft, with Willie aboard.

Twenty minutes passed, and not a word or signal from Willie.

"How come it's taking so long?" Jim asked.

"I don't know," Ken said, "he may have run into some trouble. I'm going to bring the elevator up, and go down for a look myself."

Ken punched the button, and the pulleys began to turn as the elevator started up. Ken bent over and placed his hand over his eyes. "I see Willie," he said. "He's holding on to the rope."

Willie didn't have his hat on. His right hand was wrapped around the rope above his head, his left arm dangling at his side.

His eyes were big and frightened-looking. When the elevator stopped on the platform, there was a sudden gasp from everyone. Willie's lower body was gone; his intestines hanging out, blood dripping from them. A big pool of blood covered the floor of the elevator.

"Oh my god, what happened to him," Ken said, turned away, and put his hand over his mouth to keep from throwing up. It took him a minute to get the courage to look at Willie again. He reached in the elevator and pried Willie's fingers loose from the rope, and Willie fell to the floor of the elevator in his own blood. Ken lifted what was left of him out and laid him on the platform. "Bring me something to wrap him in, Sam," he said.

"This is terrible," Jim said, holding a handkerchief over his mouth.

Sam ran up to Ken with a blanket, and Ken wrapped Willie in it. "Sam, take him to the coroner, I'll call his wife."

"Don't you think you should wait until we can get the authorities out here to investigate?" Jim asked.

"It's obvious we're not dealing with anything human," Ken said. Several crewmen were bent over throwing up, and others in shock just standing there, staring at the elevator.

Kirby turned away from the elevator, bent over, and placed his hands on his knees and stared at the ground. "I'm not waiting to get more of my men killed," Ken said. "You can see what kind of condition they're in. I'm taking them out of here now with what's left of Willie. Everyone find a ride, I want you all out of here in five minutes! We'll worry about the rig later."

The crewmen scrambled and jumped in their trucks, and were gone in the five minutes Ken had said he wanted.

"After I take care of Willie," Ken said, "I'll come back and help you find what kind of monster is in there. I owe it to Willie."

"It's alright, Ken, we'll handle it," Jim said. "Take care of yourself and your men. I'm so very sorry about Willie." Jim turned to Sully. "After Ken's boys tell the townspeople about Willie, no one will come out here, including the police. We're going to have to handle this on our own. Kirby, as bad as I hate to, we have to tell the women what's going on."

"I'm not looking forward to that," Kirby said.

"The quickest way may be to drop two or three sticks of dynamite down that elevator shaft," Sully said.

"We have to make sure it never happens again. We owe that to Chris and Will."

"I want to know what murdered my son," Kirby said.

"We'll get him," Jim said, "whatever it is."

They walked away, and the rope tightened on the elevator.

"Sully, round up the men, and send them back to the ranch to get a shower and something to eat. If there's anyone that doesn't want to come back, they don't have to. You go in to town and get all the automatic weapons and ammo you can at the gun shop. We'll meet at the ranch house and distribute the weapons as soon as you get back. I want to make sure we got plenty of firepower, whatever ate Willie is going to take a lot to kill."

"I'm on my way, boss," Sully said. "I'll be back as soon as I can."

31

The ground shook and the birds took flight. The sound waves echoed across the meadows, bounced off the trees, and continued for miles, through a beautiful July morning, leaving death and destruction on the Gettysburg battlefield.

"It's started," Will said. "The mother of all cannon barrages will be heard a hundred and fifty miles away. Now would be a good time to get to the mountain while everyone is distracted."

"I agree," Chris said. "Spot seems to be okay now, at least until we catch up to that mare."

They mounted, spurred their horses into a full gallop across a field, to the edge of the mountain, and stopped to consider their next move. "We're here," Will said, "now the hard part."

"If I remember right, the cave will be on the west slope, in a hill about a mile from here," Chris said.

"That's where we need to be," Will said.

They took off in a full gallop again, and weaved their way through the trees and brush to the hill. As they rode over the top of the hill, they saw Union solders below, being chased by Rebel soldiers.

"That's Kaman," Will said. "The Rebs don't know he's a deserter, or how much gold he's packing. Should we help him?"

"That's a tough decision," Chris said.

"We better make it soon," Will said.

"He said they blew up the entrance to the cave and they died in there," Chris said. "I think we better stay out of it and let history play itself out."

"They may be doing us a favor. If he goes in the cave, we'll follow him in," Will said.

"That's going to be easier said than done. We'll have both groups shooting at us, and we can't get out if they blow up the entrance."

"You got a better idea?" Will asked.

"No, I just don't think that's a good one," Chris said.

"It has to be do or don't soon," Will said.

"I can't think of a better plan, let's follow him in. We'll worry about getting out if we get back to our time. If not...we'll be zombies."

"That's a chilling thought," Will said.

They rode in between Kaman and the soldiers, and a shimmering light appeared and staggered the horses. For a moment they felt like they wanted to throw up.

"It's that Captain Brown," Will said.

"We made him look bad to his men," Chris said. "He's going to want our scalp. Let's get the hell out of here, I don't want to be a zombie."

"Good plan, I don't either," Will said.

They turned their horses and took off back up over the hill and kept going. Three Rebel soldiers followed.

Kaman and his men stopped at the entrance to the cave, dismounted, and started firing at the Rebels.

Captain Brown signaled for his men to stop firing. They pulled up, and he moved them to the sides of the entrance to the cave and took up a holding position. Kaman had played hell, there was no way out. History was about to repeat itself.

"Hold your fire," Kaman said. His men stopped firing. He pulled a white undershirt out of his saddle bag. "Give me your rifle, Shorty."

"Why do you want my rifle, use yours," Shorty said.

"Give me the damn rifle," Kaman said. He jerked the rifle out of Shorty's hand and tied the undershirt on the barrel, stood up, and waved the undershirt. Can you hear me out there?" he asked.

"Yeah, we can hear you," Captain Brown said.

"Don't shoot. We're deserters. We're not soldiers anymore, we have no quarrel with you now."

"You used to be, that's good enough for me. I'm sure you killed a lot of our boys," Brown said.

"We have gold, we will share with you. No need to be greedy at a time like this."

"What do you take me for, an idiot?" Brown asked.

"It's the truth. You let us out of here and I'll show you," Kaman said.

"No deal," Captain Brown said. "You're lying like all Yankees do to save their skin. You got five minutes to surrender while I get me a smoke, or I'll blow you to kingdom come. General Lee is going to have a huge victory today, and all you blue bellies will be surrendering. That's the sound of victory you hear coming from Gettysburg."

"Let's surrender, maybe they don't care about the gold," one of Kaman's men said, and Kaman shot him dead with his pistol.

"Everybody cares about gold," he said. "He won't blow us up. He'll try to get the gold and we will kill them all when they come in." Captain Brown motioned for his first sergeant to come to him.

"Yes sir?" the sergeant said as he walked up to Captain Brown. Brown struck a match and lit his pipe.

"You got some dynamite, don't you?" Captain Brown asked.

"Yes sir, but I was going to get rid of it. A bullet hits it, and you couldn't find enough of me to bury."

"You think you can get close enough to throw it in the cave?" Brown asked.

"I can try," the sergeant said.

"Do it," Brown said.

"Captain, I heard about millions being stolen by a bunch of Yankee deserters, he could be telling the truth."

"I heard about the gold too," Brown said. "After today, the war will be over soon. If he's got it, no sense in letting President Jefferson decide what to do with it. When the war's over, we'll come back and blow it out of there."

"I'll see what I can do," the sergeant said.

Captain Brown took a big puff on his pipe and tapped the tobacco out on the heel of his boot.

"Get to it. We'll cover you. It might be better if we don't talk about the gold to the others. You understand what I'm saying, sergeant?" he asked.

"Yes sir, I wholeheartedly agree. Just you and me."

"What about the prisoners?" the sergeant asked.

"Shoot them."

"The woman too?"

"She's a Yankee, ain't she?"

"Yes, but I don't feel right killing women," the sergeant said.

"She would kill you if she had the chance."

"Yes she would, cover me," he said and headed for his horse.

Captain Brown pulled the pearl-handled Remington out of his sash and looked at it, then stuck it back in the sash. He stroked his beard and smiled. "Really just me," he said to himself.

Two shots rang out, then two more followed.

"What they shooting at out there?" Shorty asked.

"Why don't you go out and see," Kaman said and pushed him out the entrance into the open.

"Don't shoot!" Shorty yelled. "I give up."

"We don't take prisoners," Brown said, drew the Remington, and shot Shorty through the heart.

"We going to bury them?" a soldier asked.

"No sense digging two graves, put them both in one. Get everybody away from the entrance now, I'm going to blow it. You can dig a hole for them after I blow up the cave. Won't be anyone to shoot at you."

"Okay, sergeant," the soldier said.

32

"I heard shots," Will said. "You think they're going to fight?"

"Not if Kaman was telling the truth," Chris said.

"I'm glad we're not there," Will said.

"Whatever that was we ran into down there made me sick," Chris said. "I still can't get my breath."

"It had the same smell the smoke in the cave did. We were too close to the entrance."

They heard the sound of hoof beats. "They're still coming," Chris said.

"I've had enough of this shit," Will said, dismounted, and walked out in the open with his rifle at the ready.

"You lost your mind, boy? They are going to shoot you dead," Chris said.

"Let's see if they want to die," Will said. He raised his rifle, shot the hat off one of them, and dropped the rifle back to his side and waited. They kept coming. They were less than fifty yards away now.

"Looks like they do," he said. "All I wanted to do was spend my summer vacation on a ranch having fun. Now look at me, I'm about to kill a man I never met."

"If he doesn't kill you first," Chris said. "You're like what you said about Custer, you got more guts than brains."

"I don't see you hiding," Will said.

"I can't, I have to keep you alive."

"I'm not as good as you, but I can take care of myself." He raised his rifle again and shot the hat off another one. They stopped and sat there, looking at Chris and Will.

"We get the message!" one of them yelled. "You could have killed us." He waved, and they turned and rode away.

"Kind of lost it there for a minute, didn't you," Chris said.

"No, I decided I'm done with it all. I'm going back to Gettysburg to get a uniform. Better to have a life, even if it doesn't last long, than to wind up in that cave forever with the walking dead."

"Did you notice the shooting stopped at the cave?" Chris asked.

"Oh no, I'm not going back down there," Will said. "They're not going to trap me in there with Kaman. If I die, it's going to be out here in the open air."

"Wouldn't hurt to take a look. Maybe they made peace, and we can go in the cave and find out how to go home without getting blown up," Chris said. "Let's ride over the hill and take a look." Before they could get to their horses, a tremendous blast shook the ground, and a big black cloud of smoke bellowed up out of the cave, with lightning bouncing around inside the cloud like a pinball machine. Will looked at Chris. "You still think we should go down there?" Will asked.

"I suppose not," Chris said. "We'll stop in Morganville and get something to eat at the diner before going on to Gettysburg. I don't think Miss Kitty and the marshal will be there."

"I don't either," Will said. "Right about now they are wishing they stayed home."

"I wonder if they became zombies," Chris said.

"We didn't see them, but there was more coming in the smoke when we were blasted out of there," Will said.

Custer pushed his head out of the saddle bag and barked.

"Okay," Chris said and sat the pup on the ground, and he peed and ran around sniffing.

He picked him back up and put him in the saddle bag. "I know you're cramped in there, but it's the only place I got for you. You can get air, you'll be okay. I'll feed you as soon as I can."

They got back on their horses, and the big black cloud moved with them as they rode away to the ravine and up another hill.

"That cloud is not going away," Chris said. "It has that smell, what do you think that means?"

"Nothing, it's from the explosion," Will said.

"There's something strange about it," Chris said.

"Like what?" Will asked. "I don't know, it just looks different. It smells like the smoke did and it has all that lightning in it."

"You see any faces in it?" Will asked.

"No," Chris said.

"Then forget it," Will said.

They heard horses and saw Captain Brown and his men riding toward them. "Looks like those soldiers didn't appreciate you letting them live. They're bringing everybody"

"Since we decided to be soldiers, it might as well start now," Will said. "We'll have to take them down if we can."

"Let them get a little closer," Chris said. "We'll charge, firing as fast as we can. They won't expect that. You work from left to right, I'll go from right to left; picking off as many as we can."

"Sounds like a plan," Will said. "This may be it, Will. I can't think of anyone better to go out with."

"Me neither," Will said.

Chris reached back to his saddle bags and tied the strap down so Custer couldn't poke his head out. "I hope you survive, little fellow. I should have left you at the livery stable."

Will rode up beside Spot. He reached over and shook Chris's hand. "It's been a hell of a ride…literally," he said.

Chris nodded, and they pulled their rifles from their scabbards, kicked the horses in the flank, and took off, like they were shot out of a cannon.

Captain Brown and his men were riding hard toward Chris and Will. "I told you next time would be our time!" Brown yelled.

The black cloud moved toward the soldiers. Lightning flashed inside the cloud. A Springfield rifle with a white undershirt tied to the barrel fell out of the cloud and hit the ground. It turned to a rusty chunk of metal in an instant. The Rebel soldiers fired, and bullets whizzed by them. They raised their rifles to return the fire, and the black cloud dropped down on the soldiers and covered them and their horses like a blanket.

The soldiers began to disintegrate, and in seconds they were all gone. The strange black cloud rose up into the sky and floated away.

33

"What just happened?" Will asked.

"I don't know," Chris said. "It was like puff, and they were gone."

"Where do you think they went?" Will asked.

"No telling. I have a weird feeling," Chris said. "My whole body feels like it's going to explode."

"Me too," Will said. "The cannon sounds are gone. The entrance to the cave is covered. And that looks like a drilling rig on top of the cave hill. I think we're home, Chris. That thing sent us back."

"Why?" Chris asked.

"Maybe it realized it made a mistake, that we didn't belong in the cave with Kaman," Will said.

"I doubt that. Kaman said he made a deal with the Devil, it may have been the Devil."

"I don't think he corrects his mistakes," Will said.

Chris hurriedly reached back and undid the flap on the saddle bag, and Custer poked his head up and licked his hand.

"He made it," Chris said. "Custer, you are the oldest dog in history and you're still a pup." He lifted the puppy out of the bag and hugged him.

"Well I'll be darned," Will said. "I never thought it would happen."

"Well it did," Chris said. "I'm glad we didn't go back in that cave."

"Yeah. But unfortunately, Kaman, and his boys as he calls them, are still running around the mountain, turning people into zombies and eating them," Will said. "We have to stop them. They're going to be a lot harder to kill a second time. We're going to need help."

"I don't know what they're doing with that rig, but I got dibs on Kaman," Will said. "I promised Jennie I would personally shoot him with her gun, and that's what I'm going to do."

"I don't see anybody," Chris said. "It looks like they abandoned the rig for some reason."

"Must have been the zombies that scared them off," Will said.

"I would think so," Chris said. "We may have to do this ourselves."

"If you're insinuating we go down in that elevator, forget it," Will said.

"I just saw something run behind that bush over there," Chris said.

"What bush?"

"The one right in front of you. You blind?" Chris said and drew the Colt.

A man rose up from behind the bush. He was ragged, with bloody eyes, a twisted mouth, and he was drooling all over himself.

"Not today," Chris said and put three slugs between his eyes. Blood squirted out of his head, he fell to the ground, and Chris put three more holes in him; he stopped moving.

Another zombie appeared from behind a tree and started toward them. They drew their rifles and filled him full of lead; he went down

Spot reared up, and a zombie came out of the ground, trying to take a bite out of him. Chris moved Spot away, and Will shot the zombie four time before he was dead.

"They're everywhere and we haven't got to the cave yet," Will said.

"As many times as we had to shoot them, our ammo won't last long. We better hightail it out of here before more come," Chris said.

They heard a voice say, "Over here." They turned to the voice and it was Kaman, holding his Springfield. "You didn't think you would get away, did you?" he asked.

"We got you surrounded. Any way you go, my boys will be there. I been adding to my army since the last time I saw you. Got a preacher, two bounty hunters, a little old lady, two boy scouts, and some farmers that thought they would take a shortcut."

"We saw you when you were alive in Seven Stars and Morganville. We got a score to settle with you," Will said.

"Don't remember anything about that, but I know what's going to happen to you now. You're going to become one of my happy band." He laughed again and waved his arm over his head, and the zombies began to crawl out of the ground all around them.

One made a run at Chris and he shot him four times before he fell.

"There's no way we can get the horses through, with us on them, without the zombies taking them down. If they keep coming, they're going to get the horses anyway," Chris said. "We have to create enough of a distraction for them to get away," Will said. "We'll have to fight on foot, that's the only thing we can do to save the horses and Custer."

They dismounted and loaded their weapons one last time. "I'll make a run, shooting at the zombies," Will said. "While they're after me, you get the horses out of here."

"Don't make too much of a run, you won't come back," Chris said.

"I'll be alright. Take care of the horses and Custer," Will said.

Chris pointed the horses in the direction he wanted them to go. "I'm ready," he said.

Will made a dash through the zombies, shooting at every one he saw, and they all followed. Chris slapped the horses on the butt as hard as he could. They took off running, and were a hundred yards away in seconds and still going. Will made a mad dash back to where Chris was.

They backed up to each other, back-to-back, and waited for more zombies.

"I think I got about ten rounds in my rifle, and the Model One is loaded," Will said.

"Three for me in the Colt, and five or six in the Winchester," Chris said. Kaman showed himself again. "Let the horses go, huh? That's alright, we don't like horse meat anyway. It won't be long until you will belong to me," he said, and that bellowing laugh poured out.

"I know we're low on ammo but what the hell, this may be my last chance," Will said. He pulled the Model One out of his belt and put six bullets in Kaman's gut before he knew they were coming. The jolt knocked his hat off and it blew away. He fell to his knees and dropped his rifle. "That was a mistake, we're going to eat you now."

He tried to laugh again but nothing came out. He couldn't get up, but he wouldn't die.

"That's for Jennie and her dad, you piece of shit," Will said.

"What's one more bullet or two," Chris said, raised the Colt, and put two more bullets where Kaman's nose used to be. The back of his head exploded and he fell to the ground, dead for a second time.

A truck came into view and ran up the cave hill to the elevator, stopped, and several men jumped out of the back of the truck and started firing at the zombies that were coming out of the elevator. Another truck headed toward Chris and Will.

"Here comes the cavalry," Chris said, "and not a minute too early. That looks like Sully's truck."

"What do we tell everybody?" Will asked.

"I don't know," Chris said.

"They're going to want to know where we been," Will said.

"I don't believe we were at the real Battle of Gettysburg," Chris said. "I think we should leave out the part about the gold, it looks like it's safe for now. That gets out, there would be a stampede to this mountain. We'll consider what to do about the gold later."

"Like, come back for it," Will said. "What were we saying about people trying to get rich?"

"I'm not allergic to money. Twenty million dollars can buy a lot, even in today's screwed up economy." Chris said.

A zombie came halfway out of the ground, wiggling his body to get the other half out. Will made a run at him, yelled "Fore," and swung his rifle like a golf club, connecting with the zombie's head. The zombie's body collapsed; his head fell off, rolled across the ground, and all his teeth fell out.

"They better get here soon. There's too many, and they are getting too close. One bite and we're gone," Chris said. "Well, Kaman won't be around to see it," Will said.

"Oh that's different. He won't know we're zombies and we won't either," Chris said.

Another zombie lunged at Chris. He hit him so hard, the stock on his rifle broke. He pulled his belt off and wrapped the end around his hand, with the buckle for a weapon on the other end.

A truck spun around, ran over a zombie, and came to a stop close to Chris and Will.

Sully got out, and four men in the back of the truck started mowing the zombies down with automatic weapons. Chris and Will hit the ground.

Sully ran up to them with his Winchester, ready to shoot. "It's Chris and Will, Sully," Chris said from a prone position. "We just look like zombies, we're alive."

"You don't look much like Chris and Will, with that beard, and you stink to high heaven," Sully said, holding his Winchester on them.

"Yeah, I know, but we're not zombies, we're alive," Will said.

Sully lowered the Winchester. "We thought you boys were dead."

Chris and Will got to their feet. "So did we," Will said. He jerked the Winchester out of Sully's hand, shot a zombie crawling up behind him, and pitched the rifle back.

"Where you boys been?" Sully asked. "We didn't know what we were going to fight until five minutes ago. What happened to you?"

"It's a long story you won't believe," Chris said. "When the time is right, we will tell you anyway."

"Have you lost anybody?" Will asked.

"Yeah, two deputies and one of the drilling crew," Sully said. A zombie wearing a pastor's dirty white collar came at them. "Watch out," Sully said and pumped three rounds into him, and he kept coming. Slim cut him in half from the truck with his AK-47, and he fell to the ground in two parts. Slim waved at Chris and Will.

Sully looked at the zombie's upper half. "That's Reverend Brewster. We thought he ran off with the deacon's wife."

Will heard a slobbering noise and turned around. "He did."

A woman with stringy long hair on one side of her head, one bulging eye, and no left arm was coming at them.

Sully fired four times. She staggered to the ground, belched up what looked like part of a bloody hand, and died.

"That was her," Sully said. "Just goes to show you, sin don't pay." Chris and Will looked at each other, and then the cave. Chris shrugged his shoulders.

The men in the trucks kept mowing the zombies down, until it looked like they were all gone.

"I don't see any more," Will said.

"Let's get out of here," Sully said. He motioned for the men to stop firing and walked over to his truck. "Good job, fellas, we got them all."

Before anyone realized it, two zombies rose up from beside the truck, jerked Slim out of the truck bed, and started chewing on him.

Chris grabbed Sully's Winchester and pumped the zombies, and Slim, full of holes.

"Are you nuts, boy? You shot Slim!" Sully said.

Chris handed the rifle back to him. "It was too late for Slim, Sully. Once they bite you, you become a zombie. Slim wouldn't have wanted that. I did him a favor."

"Well, don't do me any," Sully said. "Put Slim in the truck, boys. Chris, you and Will get up front with me. I'll try to hold my breath until we get there."

They got in the truck, and Sully fired it up and drove off.

"Are Jim and Julie safe?" Chris asked.

"Yes, they're fine," Sully said. "Will, your mom and dad are here. Kirby's with Jim on the rig, and your mom's with Julie at the house."

"What are they doing on the rig?" Chris asked.

"They're setting explosives on the rig elevator, to lower it down in the cave and blow it up. Hopefully that will be the end of the zombies. Jim said the mountain will be off-limits after that to make sure no one else gets hurt."

"That should do it," Will said. "They can't leave the mountain."

"How do you know that?" Sully asked.

"Trust me, I just do," Will said.

"I'm sorry I sent you up here. I didn't have a clue what was up here."

"It's not your fault, Sully," Chris said. "I shouldn't have been trying to ride Thunderbolt after you told me not to."

"You can try again if you want to, I didn't have the heart to send him to the rodeo. He's still here."

"See," Will said, "I told you you'd get another chance."

"Now that I've caused all this trouble," Chris said, "I don't think I want to. He deserves to be free."

Sully ran the truck up the hill beside Jim's and stopped. The men in the back got out.

Jim looked up and saw Chris and Will. He stood there, staring at them for several seconds. "Am I seeing what I think I'm seeing?" he asked.

"You sure are," Sully said.

"I don't believe it," Jim said.

"There's a lot more you're not going to believe," Chris said.

"We gave you up for dead. It's a miracle."

"Kind of," Chris said.

Jim came to him to hug him. "You might wait until I've had a bath, I smell pretty bad," Chris said.

"Yes you do," Jim said and shook his hand. Kirby walked around from the other side of the truck. "What's going on over here?" he asked. He saw Will, his legs gave way and he fell to his knees. "Is that you, Will?"

"Yes sir, I'm back," Will said.

"Lordy me, what a smell," Kirby said.

"I know, sorry. That's from where we've been," Will said.

"Where's that?" Kirby asked.

"I'll explain later," Will said. "It's good to be home."

They heard a horse nicker, and saw Spot and Rover running up the hill. Spot came to Chris and Rover went to Will.

"Looks like you made a friend, Will," Chris said and opened the saddle bag flap, and Custer jumped into his arms.

"Hi, you little bugger. Am I glad to see you," Chris said and hugged Custer.

"Where did you get that puppy?" Sully asked.

"It's hard to explain," Chris said.

"You don't know where you got the puppy?" Sully asked.

"You wouldn't believe it if I told you," Chris said.

"If you don't want to tell me, that's okay," Sully said and walked away.

"You hurt his feelings," Will said.

"Have you boys done something wrong? Are you in trouble with the law?" Kirby asked.

"No, nothing like that," Chris said. "Give us time to adjust to being home and we'll try to tell you everything."

"And how long will that take?" Kirby said.

"We don't know, Dad," Will said. "We're still in shock ourselves. We've been through a lot in the past week, give us some time."

"I think you're hiding something bad, Will. Your mother is going to be very upset if you are."

"Mr. Littlefield, it's nothing bad," Chris said. "It's different and it's unbelievable, but it's true. It has nothing do with the law."

"Let's take this up another day," Jim said. "We should be happy they're home safe, no matter the reason. We got a job to do here. I put a plunger on the bottom of the elevator that's connected to the explosives. We let the elevator down, and boom! It will blow this hill into a million pieces, and any zombies in there will be in a million pieces too. I have it remotely controlled. Sully, load everybody up and get off the hill. Kirby and I will be along shortly. Chris, you take Will to the house and get cleaned up and get some rest, we'll talk tomorrow."

"Yes sir. I don't see a trailer, we'll ride the horses in and take care of them first. Make sure you're a long ways away from here when that thing goes off."

"I will. Get going," Jim said.

"We're gone," Chris said. He held Custer in one hand and climbed up on Spot with the other.

"I'll see you at the house, Dad," Will said.

"See you there," Kirby said. "We'll call to let them know you're coming. I wouldn't want them to have a heart attack when you walk in."

34

"I don't think we made a triumphant return," Will said. "It was more like pissing everybody off."

"I don't blame them. They're looking for an explanation and we didn't have one. Well, we have one, but it isn't one we wanted to share with them because they would think we were crazy," Chris said.

"We have to sooner or later, or we'll be disowned," Will said.

"I know," Chris said. "I thought I had a pretty exciting life riding wild horses and chasing cattle. Now it seems kind of boring."

"I know what you mean," Will said. "I don't want to be a lawyer, sitting in a court room with all those stuffy people."

"I think that's why I wanted to ride Thunderbolt so bad and didn't realize why. I was tired of the same routine every day, and he was something different. A challenge that I wasn't sure I was up to, and it was exciting."

"The last week has certainly been challenging. Maybe too much," Will said. "You think Kaman hid that gold in the cave?"

"About fifty-fifty. It may not matter now, either way. When Jim blows that place up, the gold will be covered with thousands of pounds of dirt, and if it is in the cave, it will never be found. A hundred-and-fifty-year-old secret will be a thousand-year-old secret."

"You think we should tell him before he blows it up?"

A strong wind rushed by, as the explosion shook the ground, and the sound waves chased the wind across the open range for miles and miles.

"Too late now," Chris said. "Better to leave it there, anyway. The government would probably take it away from us because it was supposed to be federal money."

"I didn't want to be rich anyway, too much responsibility," Will said.

"Have you noticed that people always say things like that when they know there's no alternative? If there was any chance you could get that money, you would do it. But you said that because you know you can't get the money."

"I meant that. I'm not a big money person," Will said.

"Alright, if you say so."

"Now you're being sarcastic," Will said.

"Yes I am. I'm already getting bored," Chris said.

"You may not have to worry about it; they may have us committed when we go into our story."

"That wouldn't be all bad, we could write a book," Chris said.

"You would be the hero, naturally," Will said.

"Naturally," Chris said and switched hands with Custer.

"There's the house," Will said. "Maybe it would have been better to stay in 1863," Will said.

"Too late now," Chris said.

A Civil War Union cavalry hat tumbled across the ground in front of them, and came to rest against an old well that had been there since the Civil War. Chris and Will looked at the hat, then each other.

"Maybe not," Will said.

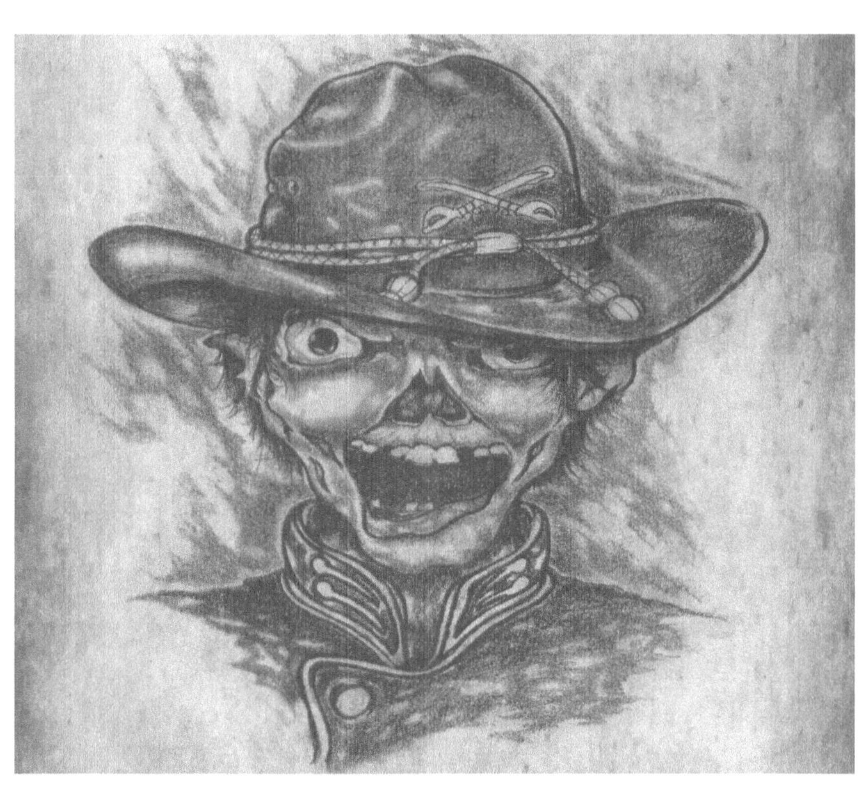

THE END

About the Author

John L. Lansdale was born and raised in East Texas. He is married to the love of his life Mary. They have four children. He is a retired Army reserve Psychological Operations Officer and a combat veteran with numerous medals and awards. Past roles include inventor, country music songwriter and performer, and television programmer. He produced and directed the Television Special "Ladies of Country Music." He has also produced several albums in Nashville, hosted his own radio shows and won awards for producing and writing radio and television commercials.

John was also a writer and editor for a business newspaper. He has worked as a comic book writer for Tales from the Crypt, IDW, Grave Tales, Cemetery Dance and several more. He co-authored the Shadows West and Hell's Bounty novels with his brother Joe R. Lansdale. He is also the author of Zombie Gold, Horse of a Different Color, Slow Bullet, When the Night Bird Sings, Twisted Justice, The Box, Broken Moon, The Last Good Day, Long Walk Home and several other titles.

TITLES from JOHN L. LANSDALE

SLOW BULLET
Army veteran Clark McKay is searching for the truth behind his best friend's murder. This search takes him across the globe, where he meets a multitude of characters and is forced to wade through the murky Washington DC waters of corruption. Clark McKay wants to find a murderer... but what happens when he uncovers so much more?

LONG WALK HOME
The O'Rourke family lives on a fading farm in the small town of Angel Point, Mississippi. With family, friends and neighbors fighting overseas in WWII - and rising racial tensions back home - the summer of 1944 turns into a nightmare of murder and loss. One boy's life changes forever after a chance encounter with someone nobody thought possible.

BEYOND IMAGINATION
An all-new collection of short stories, along with a few fan-favorites! Includes tales from all types of genres. Strap in and get ready to go to a world *Beyond Imagination*.

BOY AND HOG
In the deep woods, anything can happen. A group of white-collar workers with a hand-drawn map trek into the wilderness for a hunting expedition. But out there, will they be the hunters or the prey?

BOY AND HOG RETURN
While on patrol, two game wardens stumble onto a grisly scene hidden deep in the woods. With backup on the way, will the wardens survive the wait, or will unexpected visitors send them to an early grave?

THE MECANA SERIES by JOHN L. LANSDALE

HORSE OF A DIFFERENT COLOR – Mecana Series #1
Dallas PD Detective Thomas Mecana is on the hunt for a serial killer terrorizing the Lone Star State. Joining him is Darcie Connors, a young officer working her first murder case. With hard work, and some luck, Mecana and his partner discover a most-unusual serial killer case with murder in its very genes.

WHEN THE NIGHT BIRD SINGS – Mecana Series #2
Detectives Thomas Mecana and Darcie Connors are on the trail of a new suspect. With an ever-growing suspect list, Mecana must toe the line between friend and foe. Each action leaves them sitting in the crosshairs of danger. One wrong move could mean the end.

TWISTED JUSTICE – Mecana Series #3
Dallas Homicide Detective Sunday Verves is looking into the suspicious deaths of local drug runners when she discovers a potential suspect that hits too close to home. When the trail leads her south of the border, she enlists some old friends to track down the suspects.

THE BOX – Mecana Series #4
Detective Thomas Mecana and the gang get back together for a new case that brings back old evidence. Mecana soon finds the case bringing him back to where it all began. The latest in the horror-filled Mecana Series.

9 781949 381221